Fragments

Fragments
David Carl

Foreward / **Joseph Fuller**

Publisher / **Green Lantern**
Year / **2008**

GREEN LANTERN PRESS
Published by Green Lantern
1511 N Milwaukee Avenue, Second Floor
Chicago, Illinois 60622-2009
www.thegreenlantern.org

First published in the United States of America by Green Lantern Press.

10 9 8 7 6 5 4 3 2 1

First Edition

ISBN 0-9785756-9-5

1. Literature 2. Fiction 3. Philosophy 4. Carl, David

Printed in the United States of America

BOOK DESIGN BY JASON MICHAEL BACASA
LIMITED EDITION OF FIVE HUNDRED SILK SCREEN COVERS BY ALANA BAILEY

THE GREEN LANTERN is a 501(c)3 gallery and paperback press dedicated to the study, presentation, and
archive of contemporary art practice. As such, The Green Lantern hosts monthly art exhibitions for
national and international emerging artists and publishes limited edition books by new or forgotten
writers who are making significant contributions to today's cultural landscape. With a focus on the
visual arts, The Green Lantern establishes paths of accessibility between the work and its audience by
contexutalizing its events through writing, video, performance and music. Most recently it has joined
forced with NFP ThreeWalls to publish an annual index of alternative artspaces across the country
("PHONEBOOK") and a quarterly arts and literary magazine called "Paper & Carriage." It also co-hosts
a monthly literary podcast "The Parlor" with BadatSports. For more info, visit www.thegreenlantern.org.

Forward / **Joseph Fuller**

DAVE,

A pretty sly strategy, your not responding to my earlier missive. Anyway, I took another look at *Fragments* and, boy, was I off last time. A "crypto-relationship novel"? Of course, it certainly seems to be playing that game, but now I'm pretty sure it's a red herring. I mean really: "the membrane of language a tenuous barrier to intimacy." *Fragments* doesn't exactly trade in thesis statements, and even if it often seems like a stalled and fumbling bit of make-up sex between eros and logos, I really think that's just one of many heads on this beast of yours. Forget this "he" and "she" and their fractured colloquy, language itself is protagonist and antagonist here, and these word-lovers are a kind of thematic distraction to divert the attention so some other spooky thing can slip under the radar.

Along those lines: "The poem is not in any ordinary sense about its subject; it is an attempt to be 'the thing itself.'"

Maybe you can respond now. Just—something—a crumb or two.

Am I on the right track?

Anon,
JF

● ● ●

Dave,

Again with the silence! Are you out of town, or adding a bit more hermeneutical menace? If the latter, I'd say it's hardly necessary, especially given *Fragments'* increasingly suffocating qualities.

It's odd that the work could seem to have such a ludic spirit in one reading, and then register as a metalinguistic horror novel the next go-round. But of course I know that's not really the case. It's not even the case that this is a novel, right? I've determined pretty conclusively that it's not an epic poem, nor a philosophical work, nor anything else I can even think of. This is closer to lexical music, but where my first reading felt like an encounter with a playful jazz suite, this most recent go-round produced an impish threnody.

Patiently awaiting a reply,
JF

● ● ●

Dave,

Scratch what I said earlier. You know, I thought the whole 'authorial silence' thing was funny for a while, but not anymore.

I'd really like some kind of answer. I've interpreted and re-interpreted and re-re-interpreted and I need a little help.

Strange as it may sound, I'm back to the relationship reading. I mean this work is about something, not everything or nothing, right, and what it's about is this tragicomedy of self-consciousness. This reading I felt the tangibility of this "he" and "she" of yours—felt there was a story unfolding within this increasingly dusky wood of too many words and too many ideas. All that bothersome atmosphere of dying certitude about language is just the backdrop for these two reaching out to one another—or away from one another. Funny, before I was positive it was the other way around: they were the background, the canvas set, and the true focus was this spooky, fluctuating signal-to-noise ratio. What I haven't figured out is how to classify what goes on between this "he" and "she." Is it a romance or an agon? Is each dreaming the other, or are they too busy dreaming up themselves to grasp that the other is real? They try to escape their own minds using the only tools they have, language and more language and more language, but it just leads them into a labyrinth of solipsism and away from one another.

Pretty sure I'm spot on, but some aid would be welcome,
JF

• • •

Dave,

When we know what words are worth, the amazing thing is that we try to say anything at all, and that we manage to do so. This requires, it is true, a supernatural nerve.

and…

No variety of literary originality is still possible unless we torture, unless we pulverize language. It proceeds differently if we proceed by the expression of the idea as such. Here we find ourselves in an area where requirements have not altered since the pre-Socratics.

and...

The intrinsic value of books does not depend on the importance of its subject (else the theologians would prevail, and mightily), but on the manner of approaching the accidental and insignificant, of mastering the infinitesimal. The essential has never required the least talent.

and finally...

The more injured you are by time, the more you seek to escape it. To write a faultless page, or only a sentence, raises you above becoming and its corruptions. You transcend death by the pursuit of the indestructible in speech, in the very symbol of nullity.

Yours,
E.M. Cioran

● ● ●

Dave,

Let's try this.

Fragments has some sort of code:

yes

no

maybe
The author must keep his mouth shut when the work starts to

speak. — Nietzsche:

☐ true

☐ false

Fragments is (please check two):

☐ A meditation

☐ A novel

☐ A poem

☐ None of the above

☐ All of the above

☐ A tragedy about language

☐ A comedy about language

☐ 'David Carl' is a figment of the book's imagination

☐ _____

● ● ●

Dave,

I won't even ask anymore, so never mind all that.

A little experiment:
I decided to approach *Fragments* as something I found—a sheaf

of loose-leaf pages. I went to the Laundromat and had a seat. I picked up this stack of pages and removed the rubber band that was holding them together; I started to read. The first page slipped around to follow the last. And so it went.

Taxonomical questions fell away pretty quickly. I wasn't looking for a fiction anymore. I wasn't looking for a confession, or an essay, or a guided meditation. *Fragments* became a stroll among the ruins: it was the jagged objects themselves, the weeds springing up between them, the horizon all around. Meaning began to slip away, and it pulled even inklings along with it.

Mystery gradually withdrew as well.

Each line began to mute whatever had preceded it, until what finally remained was silence. In the end it was the white on the page that had the final say.

JF

• • •

"Dave",

Is it true that if you read into an abyss, it starts to read into you?

Just wondering, because I'm a little worried about what *Fragments* might actually do to a person. Are they predators, these lines? Is the brave, dumb, active reader essentially lunch? To read a line is to identify with it, consciously or not, a graft between mind and word, mind and image, mind and idea. And in a moment, as word yokes to word and slithers through eye and ear there is that tremor of a marriage between being and sentence. I'm thinking Pessoa here:
"All literature is an attempt to make life real. As all of us know,

life is absolutely unreal in its directly real form; the country, the city and all of our ideas are all absolutely fictitious things, the offspring of our complex sensation of our own selves. Impressions are incommunicable unless we make them literary."

And so it nests, for an instant, in the cranial dome: the realer-than-real.

The satisfaction of most writing is that we conspire with the writer on a dream of coherence: sentence follows sentence, idea follows idea, building, be it gracefully or cloddishly, into a phantom organism—a spell of continuity that reassures even if the vision is dire, because the mind simply must trick itself. It must trick itself that being is not merely a fluttering illusion, but somehow substantial, that there is tissue and ligature binding all that unruly symbolic surplus. To read is to dream ourselves into being.

But.

Then there's *Fragments*. The eye scans the line, the pupil dilates and contracts, the moment of being's birth begins—
—only to be devoured by another sentence, another blip of immanence, itself a birth, itself a death. And on it goes, page by page, procreation and slaughter, fecundity and finitude. Insidious.

A work of nullity.

A peepshow oblivion.

Or.
Is it a work of becoming?

Is this a Heraclitean literature?
Forget this notion that this is somehow a story—that there are

people hiding in a thicket of words. These teasing pronouns that recur are flypaper for being, so desperate is the reader to identify, and the moment of identification is the moment where the sentence, the phonetic cudgel, is brought down, delivering the reader a little death, so that a little birth can then necessarily come about. So let's abandon the old 'death of author' blather. This is the 'death of reader'. Isn't it?

And who is the archon rigging this maliciously tender, tenderly malicious game?

Is "David Carl" simply whoever happens to pick this up?

"JF"

Fragments / **David Carl**

To write is not to enter into an easy relationship with an average *of all possible readers, it is to enter into a difficult relationship with our own language.*

— ROLAND BARTHES

I myself only write sentences *down here. And why?*

— WITTGENSTEIN, Notebooks

"In the end, the most constitutive characteristic of the fragment may lie somewhere between the intention of the author and the approach of the reader; the former always undiscoverable, the latter always in the act of discovering."

There was no desire for arrival.

The furniture, like the weather, changes without anyone noticing.

The dwindling time between arrivals and departures drew her attention to the outdated calendar, an ancient time-map in which she had lost her way.

A constant tinkering.

She navigates among the geography of shadows.

Her fragile mouth.

Orisons for paper cuts.

Once upon a time there were any number of alternatives.

They share a chapter in the history of tingling.

He likes the circles and curves and arches of uneven thinking.

Call flesh the name of angelic letters.

Neglected ear charting for itself a course across their daily sounds.

As if by so feeding his brain some conjugal growth might visit itself upon him.

Comestible language might ooze off the page through the ravenous stretches of mind reaching out.

Vistas he knows exist and yet fails to grasp.

That the mind is but gently balanced and with the slightest nudge might topple from its isolate pedestal like Milton's proudest Satan, into a pit of knowledge unknowing.

That the alchemy of language might turn leaden thoughts into golden vistas of thinking.

Part of them emerges on the other side of something they know not what nor begin to guess its thickness.

Language laps at the edges, spills over the boundaries, washes away the barriers, and yet still they remain confined.

For example: skin and poetry.

Blood remains the most complicated language.

What about the fact that we have decided to allow the combination of approximately two dozen consonants and half a dozen vowels to represent everything we are capable of thinking, feeling, and imagining?

Thought's efforts to no longer be thought.

An obsession bordering on the religious.

No book can live up to a person's desires because books are only records of other people's desires (and whether these books stem from abundance or indigence, what one takes away from a book always depends on what one brings to it).

As if your eyes were the page on which the story of my own eyes were written.

A sphere out of control.

Harassing vocabulary.

Man imitates what he sees and is always ready to adopt desire.

What stirs.

Excitement by proxy.

He thought of her as one who bore her loss with admirable disdain.

She was feeling a bit translucent.

From the window they watch a boat floating in a muddy puddle.

All of life is a lie in response to the truth that whatever beauty does not end was never there to begin with.

A discourse that made no provisions for the future.

What she calls poetry is a certain inability to see the world.

She sees life as an affair chiefly of pronouns which she can neither order nor use in their proper relationships to people or objects.

The piles of fruit in the bowl have no mythology by which to peel them.

She threatened to continue striking him over the head with her forms of insistence until he repeated after her the words she feared to speak alone.

"If you were a book on a shelf, what two books would you want to be placed between?" she asks.

There are objects surrounding them other than the objects they have chosen to surround themselves with.

Each turned page an attempt at prayer.

Fragments on the backs of postcards sent from a dirty room in Istanbul.

Foiled by such preposterous instruments as language wields.

"You're beginning to get a picture of just how non-renewable your resources are," she says.

Shocked at the thought of barns.

Shallow without surface.

To find room for everything.

He remembers.

There were times like these that reminded them of other times unlike these.

The secret terror of those who believe in God is the fear that they are wrong; the secret terror of those who do not believe in God is the fear that they are right.

The page is the repository for an organization of words that points away from its own finitude to something more.

A full dose of the missile's accuracy.

The "long poem" fills him with fear and trepidation.

Still quivering after having been coaxed from beneath the refrigerator.

Pierced by a certain knowledge.

There was something about the sheets of plastic taped over the outside windows that lent a charming opacity to their interior world.

Below the level of responsibility an elevator starts its descent.

Bones stacked in piles along either side of the tollbooth.

Although this is not "all there is," that is the misconception that allows them to go on.

A case of one hand scratching the other.

Waiting for faces to appear at the window.

How can we articulate the notion of a structured continuum in which each part of the configuration is sensitive to the motion of every other part, however remote?

Not living as if through a continual series of transitions.

A serious work that picks up the thread of narrative and follows wherever it may lead, even to our own unraveling.

Sense of return.

Traces of a fading tradition in the dust streaked by a thin stream of saliva.

Rumors circulate like blood.

An ecstasy cannot live without devotion, some earth of basic logic.

Deep without depth.

Straightening question marks into exclamation points in order to appear more sure of himself.

Like two celestial spheres drawn towards each other across the abyss of their independent orbits, the two heads sit side by side.

The wolf and the sun are not merely different kinds of objects, they are incommensurate.

Memory held out like a rope.

She drank to the immobility of stationary things.

Her body a form of orientation around which he hovered

hopefully.

Skin sink.

His feelings died with irreproachable accuracy.

Flaccid old vampire pinned down by the vacuity of sameness.

At a certain point a man must renounce either his goals or himself.

Not *we*, but a pluralized *I*.

Locked inside the confines of his head.

She accuses him of pursuing the accumulation of knowledge.

Outside in the rain taxis sulked in isotropic spirals of isolation.

The ants were winding their way up the leg of the kitchen table.

He dried his tears on the sleeve of his camelhair jacket and fumbled for his hat in the dark as she slumped back against the light.

All one need learn from the past is that it existed.

Capable of infinite subdivisions.

To write down that storm.

If he must bear the burden of location then why not slip between the sheets of an epistemological space?

The toppling mind.

No ambition outstrips the poet's folly.

His various forms of failure his most marked success.

Whether she should weigh more heavily single words or their combined effect.

What did she know of prisons, other than what the mirror suggested?

It was the accumulation of layers that accounted for the distortion effect.

Alien genres of familiar forms.

Shared but mutually exclusive disappointments.

"Of course, there is something very permanent about death," she says.

Half mad from the absence of lists.

Dido's pyre.

Deranged by virtue of her former cruelties and not to be found among the hungry.

Tumescent words cowering under her typewriter.

The skeletal structure that frames a diverse set of impulses.

The ravenous flow of time.

He wanted to give equal weight to every sentence, to make each one the beginning of what it was he had to say.

He perfected the art of appearing lost in thought. ⟂

Objects determine the division of space.

A work in which none of the principles were named.

Fraying the selvage.

How does language obscure the depth of objects?

They say that the artist uses lies to get to the truth, for there must be a truth, which is our lives.

The peeling, fragmented palimpsest increasingly at war with itself.

His thinking hovered around the figure of a cloth-enshrouded, enormously protective thigh.
⟂

Almost like a simile.

She admired his way of impersonating someone who is waiting.

That desperate quality of words.

A certain flair for repetition.

She has come to realize that interpretations are interpretations of interpretations.

The vacuum cleaner was taking over.

His temptation was practically disembodied and kept its distance from its victims.

He tired of the futility of vain accumulation, an accretion of symbols symbolizing nothing.

Constrained to think up stratagems, they slumber on in the shadow of their mutual castigations.

All their longing stored for later reference.

The tatters of words that hover in the cemetery air.

The ground was frozen (she had only stopped to remove the dead leaves) and had soon ceased to exist altogether.

The world losing its hair and teeth lay flat and hungry before them.

 It takes a long time to be young, but it is over so quickly.

A copy of infinite patience.

A vertical journey made by mitigated victims.

The manufactured fact constitutes one of the several virtues of communication particular to the mediation of form sought by symbolic ornaments posing under the guise of bliss.

It is easy, given the context, to imagine a concrete head containing several windows through which can be viewed the immanent history of neutralized spirits.

Production forces the literal to speak a series of lies in the service of answers one hesitates to identify with the category of the real.

The interwoven growth cast shadows like a curse over the sleeping bodies of the pilgrims, tenaciously clinging to their diaphanous beliefs that floated in their dreams between the ringing bells in distant towers and the more immediate source of maternal light identifying itself as the seed of future hope.

Solid footsteps cross the threshold carrying their burden into sleep as a means of traversing the wasteland of contemplation.

Loneliness sunk in expectation of longing.

Sympathetic patterns erected painfully in the dirt by an elaborate technique of lifting the finger, closing the eyes, and plunging, without hope or foreknowledge, into the earth's flesh with every intention of allowing the results to guide them in their casting about for meaning.

Fanatically revolving in the howling linguistic efforts towards perfection they find contrary symptoms revealed as much in their embarrassing expectations as in enormous sheets of paper floating above the flames.

He wanted some confirmation of his worth from the outside world, but when the phone rang he was not prepared to answer it.

Smooth without texture.

Living among these folds of uncertainty.

Accused of the indiscriminate use of words.

It does not disappear, although she can no longer see it.

His "friend" continues working on "the long poem."

He sits at the kitchen table late at night conjugating the verb "to deny" in four different languages.

But how is one to desire without fiction?

Pain staking.

A myth that slouches off the shoulder, exposing the sultry breast below, revealing history's perky nipple.

Consider this a history of something that is happening right now.

The loneliness of the poetic solipsist.

This has nothing to do with her own form of balance, those precarious feats of equilibrium by which she keeps her seat and maintains her own great distance.

Seek ye then remonstrance with the guiding demons of your own dark genius, the impractical solitude of empty stroking hands along the smooth shell of words.

Like a game of chutes and ladders her blood moves up and down in time with the whirring of the machine's great rhythm.

She inside the machine and the machine inside her.

Words on edge hazarded less.

Reduced to a silent sitting solitary and thoughtful.

Beyond his tenuous control.

Watching her without watching as there is nothing else he sees.

The most nefarious art of style.

How can it be named save in a moment of passion?

It was suggested to her that the poet must make up her own language as she goes—but in what language was this suggestion made?

He took off his coat quietly (but was it quietly? his arms were flailing).

His arms were flailing in the corner of the room like a bird.

Cupped in words molded by the tongue held back along the shores of waste and wanton, disbelief following upon relief a mood; a sudden mood before all falls back reigning again in silence.

Wither might he dig by virtue of some prepositional frenzy: through, beneath, below, beyond, above?

Part of a larger whole which, like the curve of a parabola approaching zero, increasingly dwindles into nothing as it reaches toward infinity.

A bird digging a hole with its flailing arms while in the corner she props herself up against the weather.

Like some vampire that stirs first at dusk.

There is time are times and so full the emptiness no room even for hope left over and it is despair or comfort he can't decide rolled up on the couch cursing everything and wishing it away yet holding it closer all of it closer.

The fingers of a hand spread out to abjure the innocence of a fist.

The fingers of a hand spread in a gesture like dissipating clouds.

One of those bars where people prefer not to notice one another or draw attention to themselves.

Their sentences engender his.

They have lost all sense of proportion.

The only thing more inevitable than the future is the force that turns it into the past.

Although her methods of composition and sense-making had often led her to dabble in that alchemical process by which words are turned into people, at present she is more concerned with how to reverse the process.

Brought up short by the thought that despite all his efforts one might nevertheless come away empty handed no different from a corpse.

Are all interpretations interpretations of other interpretations, or is there an interpretation of the original event, object, or idea?

Is there ever actually a rose, or is there only the representation and interpretation of roses?

But how is one to desire without friction?

For if the journey back should prove more difficult than the initial plunge and alone inside his head no hunting ground be found, but only the whitened bones of elephants rather than the living blood of Dragons, what then?

From his encounters with literature he has come to prefer things that he does not understand because they hold forth the possibility of a future understanding greater than that admitted by present comprehension.

Did this make all the difference, and if so, what difference was it that it made?

"Do any of us touch the world," she wondered, "or is the world itself always untouchable, perhaps because there is no world beyond the illusion of our touching it?"

Her touch reminded him of a delicate membrane that swung closed like an old gate on rusty hinges before shutting him out forever.

A tool of pleasure.

An attempt to demolish the moment.

Some cards play themselves.

Months spent foundering in the cane bottom chair, waiting for the bottom to drop out.

"Maps give the impression that everything is so tidy," she complains.

To confirm herself in her chosen path by virtue of her failure.

In a closet near the door to the basement stands a mop of terrifying proportions.

When had narrative reached such a state of dilapidation?

How did she bear the friction involved in constantly moving on the surface of all those relationships?

From the window it appears as if the sun has rejoined a previous frame of reference.

We feel ourselves like a tongue bothering a sore tooth.

Frozen solitary moments preceding the heat of congress.

He knew all too well the weight of that accumulated pressure built up from years of trying to defend an identity.

Expenditure of hunters.

"Our intimacy brooks no substitute passion," she reassures him, reaching behind her back to undo her brassiere.

He could hear her whispering in his ear as his face hit the floor like a nagging question.

Had she meant to suggest that repetition, although without meaning, is nevertheless trying to say something?

The more information accumulates the less it looks like anyone is telling the truth.

Why then does memory cast such a rosy glow on even the worst of times?

She dug into what Proust called *the deepest layer of mental soil*, but whether she has true flowers to plant there remains to be seen.

Look back on the momentary absence of those words.

A poem must be more than a machine for extracting

confessions.

Desirous to lick it into forms.

Not always about placing frames around erasure.

Rewarded by an obsession.

Radiant forms.

Each word a universe.

No story here but the ones they tell themselves.

Registers of language.

They hung on every word, as if from the gallows.

Or puppets swaying on their strings.

She has only gradually come to see his giving as a subtle form of taking for which there can be no requital.

There were boats sailing through her eyes that he wanted to board like pirates searching for maps to buried treasures.

Television has become a sort of enlightenment for the masses of which they are not even aware, for ignorance and oblivion lie always at the heart of enlightenment, which seeks to raze rather than raise consciousness, which of course is precisely what television accomplishes.

Trafficking in serious dissonances.

He is afraid that she too will disappear like the innumerable first sentences of a thousand unfinished novels.

Abrasion.

Emphatic institutions rub against the wound.

A figure of speech for which there is no proper term.

Language as another subtle battle tactic.

Lost octopi wiggle smooth elbows.

Eyes ragged as a pigeon's wings.

He had arrived, only to realize that his departure was still before him.

She inserts diagonal excitement.

Without really knowing what it is she is hiding, or hiding from.

Felt by hands for all he strove to know.

His body lying firm along the lineaments.

Spectator of others.

They caught him conceiving of phenomena comical, then tragical [sic].

Beyond the ordinary rumors of mathematicians.

Nothing but the distance moving in the distance.

Busy at her fertile methods.

As larks come all is known.

The oldest metaphors meet with the least resistance.

Suspended within that second morning of consequences.

Years have accumulated like dust under your bed.

And yet to say that something is right implies that it could have gone wrong.

"Down here we like to wait in line twice," he overhears a man at the gas station saying to the driver of the grey sedan.

In line at the grocery store she overhears a child asking, "What is heaven like for those people who died before there was television Mommy?"

Breaking's just another word for nothing left to bend.

Wrapped presents and rapt presence and warped presentiments wrought resentment and wrote sentences.

She suggests to him as a definition of culture that condition in which we are all, like spiders, devouring each other, paralyzed and paralyzing by turns.

The dogs restlessly pace along the edge of the fence, the moon a distant bone.

Dilige et quad vis fac.

Their prelinguistic shadows lurk silent on the edge of meaning.

While everyone else was busy believing, she had plotted her escape from the beginning.

"I would not want to be that vicious gardener ripping flowers from the still-damp earth," she tells him.

These fingers that wrap and twine, carve initials into spines and dissect birds' hearts.

"Don't relax your grasp until you're ready to fall," she encourages.

He paused at the extent to which their identities seemed largely chemical, a series of actions and reactions, bonds, proteins, DNA, links, chains, a vocabulary of synthesis and digestion, valences, coefficients, value series, codes of identification.

Welcome to the System.

"Anyone can be bought," she warns him, "better you discover your price before someone else does."

Fissures of men.

"Everyday I get out of bed because there are books to read," she realizes.

"Sex is what we make up between commercials."

Each attempt leaves one more behind.

Her downcast eyes "the most delicate of resistances."

Each body part receives its name from the same voice.

He can feel the miracle of the written word.

The page itself, thin, delicate, a single sheet of fragile paper the repository of an organization of words (a poem, part of an essay or story, a letter, a fragment) that points away from its own finitude.

Their very material existence both the least important and the only tangible hold he has on them.

She is no longer sure that she has the talent to be a good writer or the strength and conviction to be a bad one.

She saw signs proliferate in an ever-increasing abundance around her.

Books and furniture were piled up behind the doors and windows, a mass of material which ingenious absurdity had thrown together.

In the fullness of time she came to derive no small comfort from such phrases as "batteries sold separately," and "some assembly required."

The pile of rubble became a monument to the aesthetic revolution.

"Meaning is vulnerable only to enchantment," he happens to mention.

They move casually between the pieces of long-famished furniture.

The topography of trust and superstition.

Hours spent sitting in the sun on a rough wooden bench between the thighs of an enormous building.

Unearthed by seared fingers.

Sanity such a tenuous commitment.

Contagation; lacerated tongues.

Glorious indulgence of inconsequence.

For the sheer joy of hearing the sound it made while falling.

Because it was the act of smudging that first caught his attention.

The words remained alien to her intentions.

Language plants the seeds of perversion where poetry is the gardener.

Weaving together quotes and poems and criticism and fiction to distract herself from the task at hand, which is the confrontation of loneliness.

Merely empirical; nearly transformed.

Speech's whirlpools tugging at her ankles, coaxing her downward toward the nadir of some abysmal law of form.

Every word comes grudgingly.

She called him her Hobbesian love: solitary, poor, nasty, brutish and short.

Internal aporias of the poetic muse kept passion penitent on rainy days when neither left their side of the bed but floated solitary in their union.

He left her lying naked on the floor, leafing through a magazine, and drove home in the rain, peering through the water smeared across the windshield by the decayed rubber clinging to the metal arms of wiper blades.

Whatever absence made of being.

Suddenly he realizes that he is not alone (not even in his imagination).

Shavings of cool blue ice she strung about his neck like frozen shells.

As if nothing in the world could be more remote than the awareness of their own superfluity.

Because survival had not been mandated by the creator but was rather a conceit of creation itself.

Twentieth century libraries were filled with hope for the future.

The poem has all the features of an "anti-system" because it proceeds by way of parallax.

Someone was reading poetry in a tired voice.

As if his life had become one more convention to dispense with.

A poem which is both the object of desire and the medium of exchange.

Eventually she comes to know him as little more than figment and fragment of her imagination.

Prey on the weak; pray on the weekend.

Burning the candles of her future as offerings to the ambitions of her past.

He insists that it requires more alcohol to get him where he's going not because he has a higher tolerance for drink, but because he's going so much farther.

She writes in a small room with a chair braced against the door.

Another attempt to bring memory under the rule of imagination so that the past is rewritten in a way that would allow her to regain the present.

No longer a question of what is wrong but only of what is missing.

A slice of something that might have been much larger had she not acted quickly to keep it small and fragmented.

What could be more natural than always wanting more?

The tavern is fiction, the palace poetry.

The constantly deferred promise of literature.

Shunned by cats and Heaven is a hopeless ruin.

One by one the old standards came back; though they really didn't do anything once they arrived, it was nice to have them there.

What strange symmetries align the world.

Layers in the afternoon, particles at dusk.

Her writing did not cease from calling into question the reasons why we read, from seeking higher forms of justice contingent on the rhythms of her heart which, having beat, permitted all.

The window offers a view of what they call "remarkable."

Taxonomy of albinos dancing tangos.

A bender of pens is a pen bender.

He lay at her feet like folded laundry.

Each time she consciously decides to end a line, she unconsciously desires to begin a new one.

He lies drunk and dreaming under the date palm, thinking the thought that dreamers think: "There Is."

As a result of asking too many questions the freedom she had hoped for assumed another guise.

Composition and method are both legends.

"It doesn't matter what it's about; it's not about what it's about."

By an aesthetic idea she means that representation of the imagination which occasions much thought without any definite thought being adequate to it, so that consequently it cannot be completely encompassed and made intelligible by language.

Wrapped and shot in flame, he stood within a zone of constantly shifting corners, waiting to strike.

In corners they remain cold to delight.

She enters tenseless the world.

Anonymity the reputed color of their afternoons.

How was she to read this new form of self-mutilation as a byproduct of the discourse of liberation?

He had never really developed relations with the objects of the external world.

The conveyance bearing the floral tributes is loaded promptly at the conclusion of the chapel service.

His personality having taken by osmosis something of the personalities of other beings.

Meaning emerges with a bold new assurance of its determinacy.

It would indeed be impossible for you to read these pages without understanding letters, the basic units of our language, or the numbers that make up our decimal system.

As if his body refused to reach out beyond its perimeter, refused to establish contact, but turning inward, delved ever deeper into all that lay within—even here achieving little more than a tentative union.

Even those lines that feel out of place exert their right to be there.

Furthermore, it must eat nearly its own body weight of food per day, and if deprived of food, the high metabolic rate consumes the body's reserves so quickly that in a few hours it starves to death.

She remarks that so much of what he does seems intended to dispel old nightmares rather than fulfill new dreams.

Wallowing in an aesthetic lack of clarity.

She tries to reconstruct those conventions which first enabled physical objects or events to have meaning.

It occurs to him that science is a form of literature that people no longer consider a question of taste.

A certain flair for repetition.

Eventually we all float back up to the type.

All academics are frustrated poets; but then again, all poets are frustrated poets.

The cigarette indeed is a poem that burns from one end to the other, and serves no other purpose than to burn and speed us to our deaths.

It gives us pleasure.

Breath slips from one mouth to another like the yoke of an egg passed gently between them, preserved by the tongue's caress or dissolved by the throat's convulsions.

A tongue turned playful under the scintillating touch of his evasive letters.

On her fingers danced talismans of throaty witches cackling their grandeur behind the naked sun.

Weather is only temporary.

Summer descends beneath yellow and motionless smiles.

Like toys in search of children who might break them in the

initial enthusiasm of finding out their limits.

To distill the world in the crucible of language.

Composed uncertainty.

Something lurking.

Wretchedly they waited for opacity.

The permanence of restraint.

An impossible iridescence.

The circumference pushed into position.

Wings lost in contemplating yellow.

Sadly modified.

Slow progress advancing during supernatural driving.

A light which might have been a skeleton or the door handle or his pale face in its melancholy.

A light which might have been part of a world in which everything had been reduced to information.

So far as he could tell, the more of his life he spent on the couch, the better.

Reading the most articulate form of onanism.

They spent another night yearning for that City in which the distinctions between self and other are impossible to discover.

"If you don't understand the questions that poetry asks, how will you understand the answers that reading offers?" she asks.

The silencing of that internal voice through which the very self is voided is possible only as an act of exchange within that mystic economy of a transcendent consumerism in which Marxism and Buddhism join in a church of the sublime and realize the liberating obliteration of individualism.

Not regret, but pieces of music, scattered across the floor.

They stood firmly their exploitable ground.

They kept passing the same car on the freeway, a different driver behind the wheel each time.

Form empties the glass even as she lifts it to her lips.

They line up for a chance to get what they deserve.

The genius of mediocrity.

She tries to remain within the density of a particular arrangement of words as they present themselves within her head.

He is afraid of running out, like water down a bath drain.

The membrane of language a tenuous barrier to intimacy.

The smile a coy invitation to penetration.

"Do not bite the hand that needs you," he pleaded.

As if reality were the waste product of experience.

The casting of porous vegetables before the waters of

indecision.

They keep hoping for that perfect sentence.

The savage gesture, as if gripping, imposed upon the yielding flesh.

The birds wheel past his window; the only view he claims as part of what he calls his own.

He hid the truth in the unlikeliest of places, which she invariably discovered without even looking.

Her yes is for him the condition of all language.

The past a commodity they cannot afford.

As if he were only now learning the truth of that phrase, "so beautiful it hurts," without which love has no meaning.

Why had she suggested to him that hope is what lingers beyond desire?

Any position has its limits.

Fixed meanings that prostitute intelligence.

Systems of know.

Project of not.

To clear the mind's palate by contemplating for a moment the absence of language before immersing oneself again in the forms of its totality.

Attuned to the symbolism of redundancy.

Writing too is a form of methodological doubt: its structure, its code, its system, rules, maneuvers, notions of truth, of courage, of risk and danger, belief and knowledge.

Envy for sand.

When she reads the sentence in a different context it gives the impression of having been written by someone else.

Skin sinks in sin.

A certain virtue in writing the unreadable book—to test the limits of what our ability to read permits.

Caressing each vowel with her somber tongue.

Choices that concern the disposition of time.

Closure's seduction.

The words got in the way of her mouth when she bent to kiss him.

She holds out a postcard to him on the back of which is scrawled a complete catalogue of their times.

A return to the significance, the penetration, of an appendage to which he finds himself subjugated.

An alley beckoned to him through a tangle of twined limbs.

He could feel the weeds scratching against his ankles as he leaned into the shadows for support.

He imagines a time when the couch would hold out for him the final hope of all he yearns for.

When suddenly a new era succeeds in being forgotten.

He cranes his neck over the intervening barrier in order to peer down her dress and feel terribly guilty about it afterwards.

A tangible response to an inarticulate need.

The appeal of abstract art lies in the hope that a painting that doesn't mean anything can mean anything.

"I'm not a poet, I'm just busy misunderstanding language," she confesses.

Bound by chains of easy signification.

Every sentence counts on making its appearance like the star of the show, none being content to confine itself to the conveyance of mere information.

And if no one was persuaded then that was merely another sign that she was right.

Another move towards the transgression of expression and desire.

That which might bring him into awful congress with the intimate and unknowable.

The mix grew thicker as she stirred, and soon the spoon could not be removed from the bowl.

As in music, the notes are the poem.

Every line the same with variations.

Exhausting the winds of misfortune.

What is it that she wants from language, that she has been so persistent in its pursuit, yet so ineffectual in its capture?

Her desire to keep these landscapes absolutely open is no doubt why they inevitably close in upon themselves.

Some reality must intrude.

Their libraries intertwined.

Altered to correspond.

Drawn from withered efforts.

The mind a coil wrapped around language's respiration.

Letters float in the brain and electric chemicals spell in neon the names of angels.

The philosopher ponders the purple purpose of his being.

What decorates our language like the thoughts of fleeting afternoons?

Dodging another of those minions hired by the corporations of laughter to mock her daily aspirations.

Staring down the muzzle of an unfinished thought.

Her tongue a noose for the condemned.

The sentence is his last mistake.

He moves without adjectives through the benign City's night.

What appealed to her imagination, writes Proust, *was not the practice of disinterestedness, but its vocabulary.*

Words might always offer some small consolation, she supposes.

The sentence had taken on a life of massive, albeit intimate, dimensions.

She offers him as an example of simile: "he peels words like fruit from the pages of his books."

While her tongue flickers over the shimmering surface of alien but familiar words.

The evening light had taken on a melancholy tinge, and the television could not pick up the necessary signals.

All acts of love are not cooperative.

The visible marks of their time together: the bites, scratches, and bruises which do not hurt but remain, like the writing of her body upon his own, a proof that she was here; the signature that one skin leaves upon another which cannot be forgotten even after time and space force them apart.

Progress never succeeded in flattering the independent elements of recognized forms of regress.

The essence of appropriation lies in a crude domination of proportions in which the deficient elements are a product of one dimension and the excessive elements are resplendent despite the spirit of resentment that often holds sway over the active parties.

Plural justification of entanglement if merely for the sake of excitement or adventure remains suspect despite the lapping whisper of temptation that suggests a lack which you find yourself in the grips of while at the same time promising myriad forms of tantalization that should not be confused with the images of their empty promises.

The carping of insistent voices urging one to embrace the greasy mumblings of decay amid the ravages of lascivious abandon.

When the end of night kissed the dawn of tomorrow.

Gasping through souls in the yearning not to be left behind, to be accepted into, a part of, to disappear in the whirl of that which, through participation, is transformed from other into self.

Often the advantage of poetry is how quickly it is all over.

Stampede allowances with nothing more to apologize for lying on the floor in every semblance of comfort despite the derision of passing boots blazing in their confident footsteps raining down, arm in arm, linked against opposition, seeing all at once the broad shoulders of greater evidence.

And yet somehow there is no point of contact that does not shift, no common ground that is not quick.

The disquietudes of their shared remainder.

Each day was as much like the last as the next could be expected to become.

Limits to the tenderness of industry.

He lies in bed wondering whether to salvage or pillage the few things he finds worthwhile in all his life has thus far yielded (though it is not really a decision he feels he has control over: he will salvage what he can by pillaging the rest).

Good things come in stacks, and lists arrange them.

Perhaps she thinks of books as religious objects and of certain readers as secular priests of a different system of belief and knowledge.

They say in Zen, "no amount of polishing can cause a brick to shine," or "if I could put into the poem what I feel I need I wouldn't need the poem in the first place" or "self-reflection in a polished brick."

Philosophy is only a room in the house of language in which we dwell.

The Continuing Adventures of the Sentence

She recalls the sound of his heart when her head lay across his chest.

Objects tumble into the glass.

There is a sudden undoing of buttons during which he holds his breath in the midst of a trembling hope.

Someone at the party says, "philosophy must be its own cure, poetry its own disease."

Another fall through the remainder.

Language an object of spectral orbit that occupies a solar situation in her mind; a legendary locus invoking a situational spectacle which subject to its pull reveals that there is no secular escape, no realm of resistance against collapse beneath the weight of spiritual temptations.

A verbal vacuum in which no scream is heard.

Hoping to hold in their hands a few more things while fearful, as always, for what might slip or be pried away.

One day the Original Dragon divided himself into three brothers: one went mad and took to dissipation; one pursued further division leading to the eventual generation of the earth and the heavens, animals, plants, the sea, and people; the third brother became a man and undertook the record of these events as the future would eventually betray them: he strove to become the first poet.

Eventually understanding may follow from the course and decay of natural things.

He lives in a world ignorant of the fact that the dreams of some men are better than the conscious thoughts of others.

The skin of her hands feels like discarded orange peels browning in the sun.

She is constructing a world built on the backs of others that she will find more to her liking.

The dishes remain in the sink, his motionless hands submerged in the water.

She stares out the window, observing how the days seem to pass without anyone noticing.

How did such a fabric of convenience ever become a science?

Under the threat that all is complete she tears at the edges as if to expose the boundaries of what she has been asked to accept as terminal.

He surveys her body like a miner looking for the crevice in

which to drill.

They share a cadence of liberal falling.

She stole the phrase "geological deficiencies" from someone who stole it from someone who borrowed it from the sun-cracked earth.

Words which dare not venture out beyond the cluttered souls of her uncertainty.

What is the material of any given desire?

She thinks that if her poems were ever actually read the world would explode, or worse: nothing would happen.

He imagines the long martyrdom of being trampled to death by geese.

Has she for too long occupied a room of the imagination in need of a few more sticks of furniture?

Words on edges less hazarded.

An edifice in which not to have is the beginning of desire.

The proliferation of buttons and knobs perplexes her fingers.

He struggles to contribute to the illusion of motion that other men identify with progress.

She likes the way a murderer creeps past jars of broken language, defiled tongues clacking in the yard.

He wonders at the brittleness of it all.

America is space, not time: wide-open outstretched careening distances that spellbind European envy for sand that never traced the feminine curve of rigorously scheduled hours.

Not indifferent to the persuasive power and entertainment value of coherent thought.

A cut bleeds and leaves a scar as memory erases spent desire.

Her refusals acted as an invitation when ranged along his resistant body.

He stopped to notice the way painted metal makes one jump out of beauty's way.

Beauty's sway.

What she chose to call motion others described as night descending on a solitary pigeon searching in vain for its young and its dead.

"The comfort of being wrong is that it provides you with the precise location of your current position," he assures her.

"The telephone can't ring if there's no future," she says.

No longer any seasons perceptible from the window of his freeway-driven consciousness.

The palpable City.

Streets vivisecting the City, giving it life, access, circulation.

Her sole comment on the phenomena of twentieth century media culture: "better to starve to death than be force-fed."

Through the window disagreement meets with glass.

Their observations had been calibrated to match the length of each reference point.

A case of one hand washing the other.

"What if this is love's most evocative moment?" he asks, and from it, without haste, they retreat, edging their way backwards along the cool stone wall, tracing its contours with their greedy fingers accustomed to grasping, clutching, hanging on for more.

Eros by any other name would sting as sweet.

He is about to admit his own uncertainty when she observes, "that's a good price for a mop."

He rereads each sentence as a precious example of lost opportunities.

There is a symmetry to their lack of mutual acknowledgment.

The book she would ideally write would not be written at all, but compiled.

Fingering the helpless pen.

They share the intimacy of anticipation.

Slow objects of attention float before the mind's eye.

They turned to words for comfort.

Shadows sucked along in the wake of a dwindling star.

To await the impending disaster.

A return to the natural state of mutual infection is inevitable.

Her reflections were an intrusion that succeeded in filling more of the room than she expected.

"Because what is a child but a concentrated adult?" she asks.

Whether one should follow or resist the temptation to become part of the economic–in the broadest sense of the word–framework?

Thought and language are not the same, but they are close enough to being the same to fool us when we're not looking.

She imagines that she can operate beyond grammar.

He dreams of something beyond these familiar holds, the way he'd maneuver the moving slides and bend his body around the shifting pipes that lifted and bent in the slippery light so that he might hold a crowd in suspended awe as his body moved in rhythm, in perfect harmony.

Some things cannot be faked or approximated.

He would open the silent paths of total communication, walk there himself, and induct others into their secrets.

Wheels of the passing.

Days full of what holes are made of.

Not even memory intruded on his solitude, he did not feel his body.

He longed to leave again the sphere of the material world.

A book which can never be read, but is always deferred, saved for a future act of reading, a not-yet moment of still unattained parameters.

Dialectic must be something like the final rejection of literature that embraces all language use and thus become its (literature's, language's) ultimate affirmation.

The ladder of many rungs.

Backstage, applying his makeup before the illuminated mirror, he grins at the death's head propped among the masks of comedy and tragedy.

The softening carapace around the limits of language.

The muddy tain.

It echoes hollowly but resounds with enthusiasm.

She would come across him late at night, quietly typing, at work on his endless collection of words.

A spider's offering to a closet door shut on an indifferent universe.

More and more frequently he found himself retreating into the security of frequent lists.

Her mouth moved silently around those long-unspoken words as if that once-familiar phrase might restore some diminishing proximity.

As if words could bestow the confidence necessary for final

silence.

Exploding beauty distracted by the music of flies moving through a zone of evaporation.

The very real possibility of flamingos.

As if weather were a forgery.

The Warrior, the Poet, and the Priest are all manifestations of the desire to arrange one's life in accordance with principles not readily apparent in a world of material needs and ambitions.

A desire to live one's life in accordance with often undiscovered but always believed in principles.

The discord signifies.

The bard sat at the bar waiting for that moment when sensitivity would become multivalent.

The notion of subjectivity depends on a dialectic of exchange with the text; the subject is not constituted as either isolated, asocial, ahistorical or passive, so that subjectivity emerges, develops and expands through interaction (with literature, culture, society, others, etc.) and this interaction can be enriched through theoretical insights and methodological innovation.

She found them waiting to enjoy.

At what point does the Word become an important moment in the history of ideas?

A big day for mediocrity.

"If you go out looking for signs you're destined to find them," she tells him.

A confederacy of Dueño Elegies.

It's not the boiling over that concerned him, but the sticking to the pan afterwards.

"Strive for moral transparency," she tells herself.

Or if his life amounted to nothing more than a tombstone upon which they would inscribe, "He did not strive."

To finally not know.

The psychology of the poem has its own science.

An unusual program.

He sat mired in the overstuffed chair, his mind set loose from its moorings, his face turned towards that monstrous funnel stretched out before him.

In accordance with the demands of their primitive lust, smoky skeletons march past their abandoned graves on their way to resplendent parades where they will join waving princesses and regaliaed marshals, soldiers shouldering their rifles and pilots proudly spinning mock propellers in imitation of symbolic take-offs.

An idea that begins in torture and ends fortunate in the discovery of its own efforts.

The circumference pushed into position.

She overindulges in the adventures of the involuntary.

Not death, but a diving beneath the surface of life.

She had wanted poetry as growth toward an end.

Poetry as survival of the fittest.

Jell-o with an edge.

There is no calculus of style, other than the range of the imagination, and there is no grammar for the imagination.

Experience sets limits which provide opportunities for transgression, otherwise there could be no sense of motion, and without motion, no sense of change, and without change, no literature.

It was hard for her to escape the distinct impression that this sentence had been stolen from someone who never recognized its value, and was now being offered for sale on a buyer's market where potential customers had too much respect for the previous owner's sentiment to dare make an offer.

To live means to defend a form, says Hölderlin.

The march of unscrupulous snakes.

The work must be more than a container into which the writer pours her preconceived ideas.

Not merely a record, but the very process itself.

He would allow himself to be used the way he used words and sentences from the books he read, for solace, comfort, and peace, not for hope, but to forestall hopefulness.

Magnificent the lakes and mountain villages of his romantic

imagination, swept away one by one by an increasing sense of obligation.

Insanity is less interesting than sane people imagine it to be.

But what makes it like this, ancient weights tugging at your ankles, bared skin peeled back from your smile, sitting in the sparkling light of waiting?

Shocked by the scandalous revelation of spontaneous combustion.

It's not so much that the form is incoherent as that there is no reward by which to measure the increase of understanding.

He has organized his life so that the least amount of motion yields the greatest results.

For such a complex organism it seems so simply fated to repetition.

Refracted through the half empty bottle teetering on the dark grained tabletop, the light, Newton's own child, splits and spills across the table's remaining contents: a few loose cigarettes, a silver lighter, and his own grey hand trembling over its surface.

She languishes in the liquid serenity of busy streets.

Overrun by words when there is nowhere left to put them down and no well in sight from which to draw or drown them.

He wakes in the morning in order to read his books, to smoke his cigarettes and drink his coffee, to look at pretty girls forever beyond the reach of his flesh and his imagination.

The words are a design of letters, a system for encouraging the universe.

A gardener, he sows his mind with desperation.

Replete with nothing to say but the desire to say it.

Cultural identities are constructions of asymmetrical forms of power.

"We do not exhaust anything, being more competent in the field of repetition."

She was concerned with the extent to which writing poetry was always a form of doing metaphysics.

In order to avoid being nothing more than a vehicle for shallow thinking, poetry was going to have to come to terms with a dangerous kind of experimentalism.

"When you describe the object which has many breasts, that's what I mean by experience."

The instrumentation of effective models for delineating the extension of influence on the creative process declines in the anxiety of new discursive methods.

"Yet some organizing principle must be employed, some method of election and distinction . . ."

"I too want more packaging," someone at the party insists.

No sympathy for the sympathetic imagination.

He woke with a start to find himself delivering a graveside sermon for a group of mourning relatives at an unfamiliar cemetery.

Wrestling with fate in an alleyway between two abandoned buildings.

Her writing is a way of bridging a distance that time and space create between people and events, though in order to bridge that distance she must first create it.

Trying to imagine a story that would link her reality to that of someone else.

Things keep shifting and he lets them go, words slipping like broken glass through his bleeding fingers.

If a poem cannot give as much pleasure as an orgasm, it should at least be as uncertain.

Her impoverished vocabulary unequal to the task of unraveling her confused ideas about the reality of her feelings and pleasures.

Their relationship a dedicated monument to waiting.

All they could do was pause before the brink.

She has learned that Buddhism and physics are not metaphors, that desire and entropy are not symbols.

And what if with patience true understanding does not come?

If repetition lead not to recognition?

She conceives of the moment of seduction as initiating a process of heuristic pedagogy in which reading becomes active and oriented toward the open possibility of diverse meanings rather than rejecting the page's lack of a single, clear, coherent, totalizing meaning or message.

The Albatross has a wingspan of nearly 12 feet and weights over 100 pounds: to hang one around your neck would snap it like a twig.

They groped for a fuller understanding of pleasure.

Taste is one of the most insidiously narrowing and confining forces in our lives; it divides the world into what we like and what we don't like, and hence banishes us from realms we might have judged too quickly, or never really experienced at all–taste, more than anything else we have some degree of control over, threatens to limit our world; it withholds exposure and thus experience.

They move like stones to points of rest and there lament the placid calm till passions stir them up like soaring hawks on swirling winds.

Seduction then is a form of rediscovering (and expanding) subjectivity through involvement with the literary text, while boredom is the willful capitulation of such subjectivity (the television viewer who escapes boredom not by engaging in an activity but rather by escaping the 'self' that is bored).

Spilled words breaking the spines of books, the frames of boxes, boxes of words broken across his back like angry spilling water.

Dismantling the equipment of his arrogance.

Poetry is the celebration of language's inevitability.

Bound by the subtle and tenuous cords of a mutual desire for something that has up to now remained unidentified.

He consists of atoms, confident in their swerve.

He has learned that without death there can be no desire.

Light displaces itself in favor of a tempting darkness.

A Wave and the Ocean argue over who is more fundamental.

A Forest fails to see itself.

A small animal makes plans for its escape.

He moves without adjectives through the City's benign night.

That the words spoken by the gods to men were in fact composed by poets is a claim put forward by the poets themselves, but when have the gods themselves ever asserted otherwise?

Structuring labial rollings with a jubilant splash.

Money is an epistemological system with a built-in axiological code; in so far as it provides both questions and answers it is a self-enclosed system complete unto itself.

To reopen history with the claws of time.

An anger that fluttered against his stark resistance, not allowing him even the firmness of an angry word to push against, but only the constant slippage of her tears.

Fragment (consider revising)

The constantly deferred moment of her silent recriminations.

"This common truth, if we are correct, isn't the story."

Most days he can only see things made out of letters.

She too craved the authorization of her own explanatory powers, "we do not live without reasons," she could have told him.

Memories can be so perfect.

If only the present could forget itself as easily as the past remembers.

"After the first attempt your form goes and your elements return."

Information is only interesting if you can make a choice.

How many teeth does it take to make a grin?

They articulated their romance by means of a non-cumulative language which promised to leave no remainder when the time for parting came.

A dramatic situation is always heightened by breaking off the dialogue to look out the window.

He stood before her full of apology and desire.

What difference whether something was real or read once it is over?

Accidental encounters of necessity and thought.

They border on invincible.

Desire is a mirror reflecting the world in place of our own face.

She suggests to him as a definition of growing old that morning on which one wakes up and says to oneself for the first time, "yesterday was better than today."

It may be that language itself is responsible for the fragmentation of our outer world, but it may also be the case that it is this very language which joins us to these fragments in meaningful ways.

They try to develop a sensitivity to furniture.

After the first purchase the rest flows easily, remorselessly.

Only victims seek to ascribe blame, the guilty are already busy writing exculpatory counter-narratives.

She told him he was losing his marbles, to which he replied, "at least marbles can be found."

For weeks he came daily to the park to read amid the swirling dust and shimmering inexactitude of dull green chairs that burn to the touch.

She suspects that mediation always involves some form of dissolution.

To say that the wind howls, moans, rips, tears, bites, caresses, beats or slaps is more a comment on literature than it is on the weather.

If only there were more than the contingencies of communication to bind them to the world.

When she looks back at a year in which she has written little or nothing she feels an emptiness and desperation spreading out from the past, threatening to engulf the present.

He seems to be sitting quietly with his eyes closed and she cannot say whether he is asleep or lost in some private reverie.

From his (temporary?) position on the floor (more comfortable with every passing pair of shoes) he releases the flower's shadowy eagerness to envelop the dawning mine-swept field upon which battles rage and flags unfurl, heat rising against the bones of naked joy.

Next comes the summer's last surrender at the yawning mouth of winter's door.

She tools all knowledge for her sphere according to the light of reason.

In the economy of his imagination, each word is a universe the sentence seeks to constrain.

Raising itself in unruly unison, the poem lifts its head gently from the pillow.

They can hear the glass shimmering in its pane.

He pulls socks over the ankles of false experience.

The edge of light tips the scales of a receding idea.

Literature is that great catalog of experiments and investigations into how language might expand or expose the soul.

Mistaken shirts line the streets, pausing under streetlamps to light cigars.

They live inside the perplexity of shadowy convictions.

The story of a wandering opinion and its quest for certainty.

He felt certain that all he'd ever wanted was contained in one word that ever eluded his long hours of restless searching.

Life's sense of urgency recedes with the growing sense of meaninglessness that accompanies the uncertainty over where a sentence is going.

The passion of literature is the harmony of the body and mind brought about through language.

Through her he learns to negotiate the status of the natural.

Roots and boles plunged in their temporary eternity.

Each step brought him closer to understanding his sympathetic harmony with those first amphibians who hoisted themselves up from the primal slime under the delusion that someday supermarkets, minivans, cinemas, fashion magazines and shopping malls founded on dry ground would provide them with a better chance of gaining whatever it was they sought.

In grammar, as in love, it takes two for there to be a we.

What must he defend himself against?

Rocks and stones, the limbs of trees, ignorance of self and others, the very desires that prompt him on.

As quiet as a cat appealing for forgiveness.

"I understand subjectivity as the experience of what it is like being me," she said.

They're seeking a work of art which through its fragmentary state achieves a kind of, or reveals a glimpse of, wholeness.

But how can he hope with words to unlock the mystery of other words?

Writing which is the search for mystery upon mystery and words within words.

Worlds within words.

The body tells him what he knows.

As if there had been a plan abandoned.

She waited to see where the words would take her before she began to imagine where she might be going.

As is so often the case in love and poetry, their joint discoveries were of mutual frauds and false disclosures.

Knowledge harbors unknown secrets.

A version of the American Dream no one had fallen asleep in time to have.

Writing desperately in order to still the savage passage of time and silence the internal dialogue that chained her to herself.

It occurs to her that with a little effort she might edit herself out of existence.

This was obliteration through the word, pure and simple.

Subdue the ravages of awareness.

Desperation sets its own terms of acceptance and failure.

It looks tempting from across the table but he dares not stick his fork in it.

Intellectual orifice hoping to provide a moment of instant gratification.

Their plural velocity away from the interior.

Her touch communicates to him from a source more intimate than the body.

Most of what she takes for signs of encouragement have come from under and through a dead layer that reminded her of something else.

He defines ethics for her as "the science of assessing the likelihood of getting caught."

A part of our lives each of us must live outside ourselves.

Out of letters.

So crowded here there's no room for the imagination.

The wilderness has a mysterious tongue which teaches awful doubt, observes Shelley.

From his vantage point on the front porch his view begins to make sense of the surrounding area.

"I know very well I could not be happy knowing everything," the woman says to the back of the retreating man, the axe fallen clear of his fingers.

She now knows with what she must come to reconcile herself: this piece of pie is the whole pie.

She began composing her first poem in the daylight of a child's playground, and by nightfall all the words lay in a wrecked heap about her chubby knees.

As if the movers had come to carry off the furniture of his mind while the upholsterers were still at work.

In the poem there lives a transcendental buffoonery.

"Ironic threnodies," a phrase she stole from someone else's book jacket.

Nothing astral left in his bag of tricks.

"What if language doesn't correspond to the facts of the world?" she asks.

What if there are no facts of the world outside of language?

Too early in the morning to initiate a direct interrogation of his cognitive status.

She wonders how the act of typing has gradually modified the way she thinks.

His refusal to answer the phone provides him with the simplest form of diplomatic immunity.

As if culture were something he could be vaccinated against.

She seeks a model for what she wishes to write, but secretly fears that the discovery of such a model will force her to change her ambitions, since what she most desires is to write that which has no model.

Although we struggle to disturb the mind, the ancients tell us that the brain should remain undevoured.

She wakes to her daily struggle with vocabulary.

The fragment emerges issuing great shouts that draw attention to itself while distracting the observer from what it fails to do.

She struggles to free herself from the impression of being held between violet bands, naked in her mouth and suffering from the constipation of prophets.

Dedicated to the collection of a series of sentences which even so cannot free her from the web of language.

The empty refrigerator is more than just a sign of nothing to eat; it is a sign of no one to feed.

He was plagued for years by the memory of women with blonde hair wearing blue dresses.

Each arm reaches the length of its own extension, while wanting, no doubt, to grasp at something more.

She saw in the book something like the last resort of those whose taste exceeds their ability.

The equivocal manifesto: what is it? lacking any sort of dramatic action, it is not a play; it is not a novel or short story as it has neither characters nor plot; not a poem as it lacks any attention to rhyme, meter, or poetic imagery; not a myth, fable, or allegory; not a work of philosophy for it contains no sustained or developed idea, not a journal or piece of criticism for it is not about anyone or anything; it neither confesses nor remembers anything; and yet it is a piece of writing.

They stood side by side upon the platform of the irascible.

Her arms, more than ordinary conscience, soon obliged him.

They spend most of their time on the couch, watching shadows pass by outside the window.

Where so much noise is noise no longer.

Art is an act performed with the intent of excluding the necessity of imposing criteria from the outside.

He felt her desire to heal the text of imagined ailments, diseased progeny of a disrupted mind, the fecundity of synthesis.

It may already have occurred to some people that human beings simply have a surplus of consciousness, and all this metaphysical talk of lack, void, abyss, angst, nausea, *Weltschmerz*, or just 'something missing' is merely a reaction to this over-abundance of self-awareness which we would probably get on far better without, and which many of us, who lack in proportion to others such an extreme degree of it, no doubt succeed in doing, and that the phenomenology of the poetic interlude reflects an opportunity buried under the awareness of transpiring events just beyond the boundaries of ordinary consciousness, evoked by a momentary recognition that what is most vital in the realm of human activity is often least likely to receive significant expression in the flow of quotidian events, whereas this revolutionary moment battles perfidious elements in the dehumanizing social sphere which we have come to call ironic with a bitter undertone due simultaneously to the fact that it is we alone who are responsible for this society and we alone (along with the planet itself and every being and creature on it) who suffer from it.

Neither passive expectancy nor energetic activity are appropriate in this new sphere of interaction between human beings and what we have begun to suspect is the destiny of our combined fears and desires.

Nature, phenomenologically speaking, did not exist until created through perception; hence art returns us to Berkeley's *esse est percipi*, and also reveals the fundamental solipsistic nature of each individual's experience with art and the world.

The mind flows remotely.

The length of better advice.

Directions in space amended.

The code of ammunition.

Poetry is the seduction of isolation.

True freedom is not the ability to fulfill our desires, but the ability to discover desires that are truly our own.

She started making a list, and she couldn't stop; she kept adding to it, night and day, and she couldn't sleep, she had to interrupt her eating, her conversations, everything she did throughout the day; in the middle of watching television, while in the shower, during sex, she had to keep stopping what she was doing to add to the list.

Reflections on the sentence in the form of sentences.

Television embodies an effortless manifestation of remaining in the present tense.

It took him a long time to realize where he came from.

Where do the meanings of words go after the words have been forgotten?

The better writer she becomes, the fewer words she uses.

Did they pray for or dread that satisfaction of desire which is also its end?

What writing prose sonnets reveals to her about the cold of amputation.

He watches her cross her legs.

All diligence in chains.

At sea in the process of articulation.

To what extent is the poem a surface onto which we project our desires and expectations?

The wind from the fire has blown his tattered books into the yard, where loose pages flutter like fallen angels.

The burnt pages like blackened snowflakes melting in his fingers.

Bottles of wine mire themselves in the dirty carpet.

Laughter is its own redeemer and clears away during the moment of its occurrence the myths of good and bad necessary for the existence of society.

She suspects that his excuses have become confessions.

Writing as a process of alluvial condensation.

Boredom is the absence of desire.

It is best to practice virtue without believing in it so as to compensate for all those who believe in it without practicing it.

He can feel the words like fingers prying at the closed edges of his mind.

Calling something calls it into being; it exists because we have named it.

A poet's words must serve their purpose in defiance of natural expectation.

A light shows but nothing seen is revealed.

Groping all the way.

Certain problems which were not a part of his soul, others that were.

The sentence might become more than just another opportunity to arrange words according to a novel yet predictable order.

And the world behaves accordingly.

And yet it is necessary to admit, if only to himself, that whatever it is, there's more than books between him and it.

One by one, as the books are removed from the shelf between them, a gap grows through which they might eventually come to see one another.

She shudders at the lewdness of meaning, infinite or frightful.

Among his forms of botched infinity resides that space hollowed out between understanding and the dismissal of those same infinities.

In his hand he holds a package of flexible cheese.

Writing lies in the process of elimination.

Dampers from the dismembered piano dangle from strings attached to the ceiling.

A sentence constitutes a complete interior event from which she furnishes her mind.

At night he held the thought of her to his thin chest until he could feel their bones begin to merge.

A fragment is not so lonely as they would have you believe.

You strive to apportion pleasure, to squeeze punishment of its final eloquence.

A kiss that strives to thrash the barrier erected by the mouths of isolation.

The place of utterance is crossed by that which cannot be sufficient unto itself.

"Your abstinence constitutes my orgy."

She kisses back, hard, and you push her up against the closed door, out of sight of the window with your hands up her shirt, hence fascination with the discrete sentence as a unit of reference.

From the window he watches the weeds in the backyard growing through the broken bottles and discarded volumes of ancient writings.

Something lurking out there.

What they catch with the skillfulness of words falls short of what they aim at.

When he was a child well-meaning relatives and family friends would ask him what he wanted to do with his life, and although he did not fully understand the question, his answer, "I want to read a poem," was delivered in such a way as to invariably produce in his interrogator a look of confusion swiftly followed by gradually dawning terror which typically led to them hurriedly backing away while casting glances toward the nearest exit, as if that door (or window) might suddenly slam closed, leaving the well-meaning questioner alone with this unruly child.

A secret ubiquitous presence throughout history and culture has burrowed into her mind.

He was having a hard time keeping track of his status, apropos that hook which he was sometimes on, sometimes off.

In time the museum itself became the location of a series of explanations about the purpose of order as a means of conducting history.

The hospital remained unchanged from the beginning of his visit until the end.

His side of their conversation constantly adapting in an effort to keep up with the contortions of her facial expressions.

Heroes need rhetoric too.

And what would her excuse be for laughing at his excuses?

Separating each word off from the whole for future consideration.

As if literary tourism were nothing more than excitement by proxy.

Some mornings he wakes up unable to find his bed under the pile of books that has accumulated there overnight.

In the glory of her mathematical imagination she can go for days subsisting, like an ethereal plant, on light alone.

Because of the nature of its relationship to language, true writing is more about discovery than about expression; about how language might reveal us to ourselves rather than about what we might use language, as if it were some transparent medium of expression with no substance of its own, to show others.

Art is defined by reaction, not by action; it is a phenomenon of recognition, not of creation.

The poet struggles to open up a space in everyday discourse where a moment of recognition might be possible.

Art is the attempt to create the potential for experience.

In his imagination he is reading a novel about his imagination, or perhaps it is about his lack of imagination.

The reader runs all the risks in literature because the writer allows the reader to take liberties that she must deny herself.

In his newfound confidence he finally feels ready to confront the resigned pretzel resting on the bar with an air of finality.

She would like to frame her narrative, and then frame that frame, and so on, so that there was never a picture, but always a series of frames, each stepping back as if to get a better perspective on something that might not even be there; she would like to write an endless series of descriptions of the work she would like to write.

Chess too is about lines, where to cross, and how, differentiation, skill, hierarchies of talent and ability, strengths and weaknesses, knowledge and ignorance.

Systems of knowledge, axiologically laden codes of belief and behavior.

He found himself reaching for the gun on the bedside table with increasing frequency.

Knowledge of secret systems, private languages, codes, the mysteries of power.

Delighted by the childish miracle of an incomprehensible world.

You come to terms with them in your own territory.

Can there be a reading of the text which is not a form of co-authorship?

Each sentence is formed from a combination of relinquished and unrecoverable souls.

Something changes in the world, no matter how completely words fail to record that change.

She struggled to rescue the image from a theoretical environment which seemed to want to enlist poetry in the service of something else, as if to make poetry teleological.

She saw how the world would crumble around him before he noticed that he was alone in his enthusiasms.

His room constitutes the revision of an imagination.

Modes of know.

The technostalgic age.

The past a commodity in which we still have room to think.

A lifetime of discretionary pleasures.

Counting their money in his thin cool.

Floating eyes above the surface of the water.

Waiting for her with his belt around his neck, his knees quivering.

The light hurts his fingertips as he turns the bulb.

She realizes that man is not the measure of all things, but the measurer.

Colonized by a philological model, a pure mythology of language.

Agenbite of overbite.

Although the words in each sentence build upon each other, the combination of these sentences does not go anywhere.

They are already here; their desire to skip ahead, to get to the point, is foiled.

Writing is wages received from the diabolical powers one has served, writes Kafka.

The better he becomes, the less of him there is.

Not trammeled in the repulsive dryness of dull antiquity.

How did her words manipulate his desire to understand?

Not history as it really was, but history as they now see that it must have been.

How little one actually needed became apparent to him only after that too had finally been taken away.

Her gesture reminded him of those days spent in a small Mexican fishing village waiting for a bus that never came.

The vast unknown.

Later he finds himself on a bench, hands cupping his face, subject to these prose visitations.

Pummeled by the drift of solar abandon.

The match flared in her yellow fingers and the flames leapt around her suddenly certain hand unshaken for the first time in months.

Books may be one of the last remaining proofs that the human mind is still an integral part of the human being.

He imagines that as the end approaches they will either not be around to see it, or they will still be so involved in recovering from the beginning that it will hardly seem to matter.

And yet she remains, incomprehensibly, eager to please.

He lives in the madness of first causes.

The voice coming from the television warns them of the limits of dawn and evening.

She sees it all lift up around her, lift up in one glorious flashing moment before falling darkly as she knew it must.

He considers the possibility that ignorance is its own reward.

Reading out of a sense of obligation to some unfinished task that lay before him (a task that in many ways he came, eventually, to identify with himself).

The voice reminds them of a man locked day and night in a cellar until he has forgotten even the memory of a light he once took for granted.

What it means to live in a place that is not our own.

They formed their memories from the brittle intoxication of unspoken sentences.

Sagacity of dearth.

It is when two of the most dangerous forces in the world—human physical desire and the ego's insecurity—are coupled together, that we find men and women treating each other most cruelly.

He fights off the sudden impulse to run, to throw his body through the window in an effort to purify his flesh in a shower of broken glass and remorse.

Cacophony of the drunken pilot.

In her darker moments she sensed nothing beyond her awareness of how life contracts and death expands.

Constrained by that vague and elusive wisdom not to be confused with truth or misunderstood as something useful.

Presented with a series of vague propositions leaving her stationary in her freedom even as they move through the dull moments of her servitude.

Presumably the ways of investigation, the head on the night table, the act of interpretation, the practice of emptying so that the body walks forth naked, were linguistic experiences common to all the participants.

The existential discord of experimental magnification makes us think that solving the problems of consciousness involves the orbit of smaller bodies in forfeiture to their original purpose.

A Sabbath of spontaneous production during which the knocking about of repeated ideas came to be heard as words syncopated by the suspension of our thinking.

Earthly passion is something like the unattainable peace for which we long while an infinitude of possible frustrations prowls among the secrets by which we thought to protect something of ourselves from the original assault that first lost for us that other garden.

The price they are willing to pay for an insight into the nature of sensual intuition confronts them with the explicit demand that they devour that which repulses them without disparaging their original appetite or castrating its potency to offend.

The dictionary itself could not provide us better guidance.

With a roof under which to hide our luggage and scattered candles casting an alien light into the compelling night we huddle on the bed a few inches above the rising water, the pillows towerlike in their piles, the blankets purled about our ankles, the windows shaking back at us the echoes of frustrated gratitude.

Happiness is a popular model.

Devouring the American joke as an ersatz for exploitable ritual.

Sensuous imitation illuminated the equivalent values.

Power intensifies the force of tattoos congealing over the brittle hopes with which we cloak our skin.

For over 20 years she's lived with 30 words and bent them to her will.

"Do prepositions mark his world, as they do mine, with signs of absence and betrayal, the disappointment of understanding objects in their places?"

Having shown some of the deeper recourses to which study will go in order to assert its claim as a legitimate form of cultural pleasure.

Prehensile tales.

What was it Fanny Howe said about Virginia Woolf and Simone Weil, that they had *sought salvation in a choice of words*?

To write, that is, to create something in language; or had she been approaching the problem in the wrong way?

Lists are verbs.

Skin glistens with sweat during the creation of her own image.

What was it Wittgenstein said about it being *humiliating to have to appear like an empty tube which is simply inflated by a mind?*

Self-enjoyment is the enjoyment of something else.

A sudden shift in attention seems to change everything.

She notes how in conversation with friends her use of language often seemed spontaneous.

What was it David Jones said, that *I have run a hand over the trivial intersections?*

Deceptions can be deceiving.

A story in the ascendancy of ideas.

Insight is no longer constitutive of those forms of art assigned the task of giving pleasure.

Aesthetic hedonism is a series of facts deprived of their ability to refer productively to the forms of motion most commonly found in the sensuous world.

"You are dismissed as delirious and nourished in the vast machinery of sin," suggests a voice on the radio.

Low remorse vibrated on the horizon.

She wore nothing but a distribution of shiny silver stars draped on long gold chains.

In order to renew this archaic view and begin again.

The sky cracks open and the air like syrup runs through her

hands.

By virtue of an ivory indifference the cloth pills beneath his thumb from too much rubbing.

If narrative mirrored sound she would not grow weary in its echo.

A process of dismantling the vestiges of their residual personalities.

Conflagration of reason.

To fill these hollow places.

The things outside themselves.

The perception of space that corresponds to their perception of time is the interpenetrating and superimposed transparency of the world.

Through his neighbor's window, thrown open with abandon, he stares into the still restlessness of day's encroaching threat.

Am I a metaphor for history, or is history a metaphor for me?

Stuck as if in mud not to be shaken loose but which must be dwelt in and dealt with.

One never went quite far enough when it came to establishing the best possible refuge from the future.

Over their shoulders the past still there.

If a thin or plated Body should be broken into fragments of the same thickness with the plate.

The hours wend their way to nowhere, where they will eventually find us waiting for them.

Stop in the still moment of sensual delight long enough to forestall the longing which haunts you in the memory of another's embrace.

Finally, the light hurts his eyes and still he's afraid of the dark.

No longer blind to the threat of insight.

The wind, in similic beatitude defying metaphoric categorization stirs the dust and whips leaves into a frenzy of disorder and through this vortex she peacefully dances.

The sentence is one of the fugitive parts of literature.

From the window she watches how form wavers on the brink of content before taking the plunge.

Feeling small and frail amid these robust occupiers of space.

They caught her impersonating a meat-colored baby while trying to sneak into the hospital's forbidden library.

He prefers staying at home to going out in public places where no one knows him nor has any interest in doing so.

"Why can't I beat my head against that wall?" she asks.

A bout with aboutness.

Temporarily enraptured by the multiple possibilities of plagiarism, she was captured alike by the fascination and intimidation initiated by her encounter with Klee's *tremendous fragments of meaning.*

Toe express.

Inspiration covers shifts in makeshift intuition.

What expectations does the mere presence of the sentence provoke in us, and how, in turn, does it employ various forms of subterfuge to undermine these expectations?

Like the taut belly of an oceangreat whale the car moves blue through the moonlight gliding on silent rubber fins.

In hopes of rediscovering that America which had managed to remain a desert without history.

He sees that the number of stuffed birds populating her room has increased, as if they had learned to breed in the face of inanimate improbability.

She took her readings as if from a barometer of thought.

Amazed at the lengths to which writers would go in making up scenes and scenarios, plots and characters, places and times, events and objects, all in order to talk about themselves.

To persist is the key to being.

How then might he free himself from these various modes of intellectual terrorism in all their forms of libidinal recrimination: formalism, phenomenology, structuralism, psychoanalysis, Marxism, Positivism, Nihilism, theology, Buddhism, Vedicism, stoicism, skepticism, humanism, existentialism, socialism, realism, surrealism, mysticism, post-structuralism, cultural criticism, Vorticism, post-colonialism, new criticism, romanticism, hermeneutics, Situationism, Angry Young Manism, Absurdism, new historicism, classicism, Futurism, the renaissance, enlightenment thinking, dialectics, Fluxus, semiotics, semantics, anthropology, aesthetics, ethics, epistemology, eroticism–each in turn divorced from redemption.

The ultimate value creates a demand.

Intentionality will already have become internationality, and referentiality will look like preferentiality.

A bad day for elevation.

The flesh is sad and the seagulls are drunk.

A flower lifting off its stem and crossing the sky like a yellow cloud driven before the wind.

He felt betrayed by a culture which had left him with no name for that desire which resides outside the matrix of sexuality and materialism, and hence with no way of calling to that which he needs most.

"Meaning is more than just a question of waiting until the lights go out," she says.

He harbors his own sense of variation that he hopes to express in respect to a given act of satisfaction against the limit of some understanding abruptly withheld.

The absence of taste is no substitute for intolerance to ambiguity.

To be rewarded for an obsession, maimed and quivering.

She sought an expansive response to, rather than a reductive explanation of, the world's dense objects.

We fashion our attitudes out of misconceptions about our

circumstances.

"Lyric cannot be expunged by modernism, only repressed," she says.

Reading requires an interrogating and critical mind that can nevertheless suspend interrogation long enough to go on faith when confusion sets in.

Seated on a park bench over the course of long afternoons she keeps herself busy with the ceaseless composition of lists and catalogues, of commonplace books and fragments, a dictionary, encyclopedias, atlases, a book of anatomy, parables, anecdotes, song lyrics, quotations, remarks, meditations, recollections, memoirs, letters, observations, notebooks, and lists of lists; she keeps herself busy, but can't help wondering what it is she's hiding from behind all her busyness.

A completed thought is as good an excuse for giving up as any.

"This too is part of the Opera," she says.

What then is the relationship between language and meaning? is there meaning already present in the world before language, or is meaning something that only comes into being after language is there to interpret it?

"This is the poem I cannot write; a form of letting go I cannot do."

When she spoke to him that final time promising, "from this day forth I will forge with you my memories" and then never saw him again, shouldn't she rather have said, "I will forge you with my memories"?

She believes in the poverty of desire.

Part of the hope they attach to aesthetic resurrections.

The nature of reading is incompletion.

Caught up in the effort to fill content with its own lack.

Defying time is a vast expanse of dialogues, lectures, novels, aphorisms, notebooks, poems, investigations, discourses, sermons, dramas, confessions, cantos, fragments, philosophies, elements, stories, fables, meditations, maxims, essays, letters, journals, ideas, and reflections in the form of words; really they are all fragments, not even sentences (like music, which always comes in pieces).

Defying time but ultimately defeated, for she cannot avoid the thought, "now I have 30 more years left," and then, "now I have 20," and so on until there is no more thinking to avoid.

Without love there is no end of desire, but even with love there is still no end to desire, so we must learn to live with desire.

He occupies himself by breaking loneliness down into categories, in much the same way that Dante described the various circles of Hell: there is the loneliness that waits, fastening the telephone, the door, the sidewalk in its wavering gaze, hoping to glimpse some trace of relief—a loneliness that waits suffers the torment of expectation; but far worse is the loneliness that does not wait, the forsaken loneliness of despair that bears no hope, for while the first loneliness seeks comfort in the past, this second loneliness finds there only bitterness and mockery; in the worst of lonelinesses there is no volition: love violates the subject, rendering him a victim of the very emotion he thought to seek solace in.

Meaning is a system of difference, but change simply a matter of repetition.

He saw that it was his fate to live in a state of passive blindness regarding the ways in which an understanding of the needs of others might have gone some little way towards the fulfillment of his own.

The mind a cup that was emptied long ago.

He held gently, as if in fear of breaking them, the records of her beautiful dinosaurs.

Where then the lines we draw, and where the sand in which to draw them?

The place of dwelling is for the first time opposed to the place of work while his living room remains a box in the theater of the world.

Despite all evidence to the contrary, the wings like flames cast shadows across the carpet.

She longed to write for him one of those sentences described by Proust as, *sentences which dropped into his heart and turned at once into a solid state, grew hard as stalagmites, and seared and tore him as they lay there, irremovable.*

Long hours he sits alone with her in his room, promising himself, "when this candle burns out I will kiss her," before lighting another and finally the light comes up in the morning sky, his last candle lost to the day's brightness.

Nostalgia too has its own private language, its system of values and signification, the language of gorgeous phenomenon, scrotum catheters, undiscovered bounty, jubilation and exhaustion, old loves, or their memory, which outlasts.

"I can't give you what you want, because it isn't me you want it from," she tells him.

What kind of a way is that to take your revenge on literature?

What in the end comes first, the ideas, which submit to words, or the words themselves, which lend an air of material existence to the ideas?

Of Shakespeare Dr. Williams tells us, *by writing he escaped from the world into the natural world of his mind.*

He waned.

She heaved the pen off the desk; if she were nearly finished there might be some consolation in pressing on, but there was no end in sight, anymore than there had ever been a legitimate beginning.

She asked herself what emotions these were that coursed through her veins at the sight of him, as if music was being played on her bones by a flood of coffee.

He fears nothing so much as waking up one morning and looking out the window with no expectations, seeing nothing but empty days ahead and empty bottles behind.

She insists that Paradise, although we have no earthly value save our own lack to attach to the word, will still be worth exactly the price we demand to pay for it.

A fox with a hedgehog complex.

"What is the position of real desire?" she asks.

Heap the words: are they the tower by which you will climb to your destruction, the heights you must scale to reach your downfall?

They hear the insistent voice repeating, "yes, but it's a dry heat," as if this were some kind of consolation.

While changing it rests.

If happiness consisted in the pleasures of the body not a sound would be heard except for the dripping of a water pipe buried in fallen leaves, and the sex appeal of the inorganic would be its vital nerve.

Is reading the gratification of desire or the beginning of it?

We have satisfaction in proportion to our ignorance.

Not even watching as he plucks those floating pages out of the storm.

Explosive fingers glide across the brittle pages of neglected books and ripple with anticipation at their unexpressed ideas.

The Poet was a citizen of her own language, but with no one to speak to it became a desperate citizenry on one, the nationality of solitude.

The linguistic equivalent of a cyborg: part biology, part grammar.

Your toe stands coughing?

Her problem lay in the fact that she persisted in feeling as if unhappiness wasn't about what she did, but about what the world did to her.

Parking is such sweet sorrow.

Just another mote in the beam of pleasure.

A little neglect goes a long way.

Frames, disruptions of text, articulation of desire, absolution from the wide-open portals of your mind.

Akin to the captive audience of repetition.

Even the Hegelian sponge cannot wipe clean the slate of history without leaving a few streaks.

So much seems to depend on personality, and it seems as if so much can be explained by it–but then what does personality depend on, and how do we explain that?

Your toast and coffee.

A case of one hand watching the other.

Even now was ahead of him he was so far behind.

A mirror is not a dream but rather the frustrated desire to produce that stares back through feeble fingers held to eclipse her empty features.

She senses that language was created to make poetry possible, which art, long resentful of its parent, has sought its destruction ever since, which cannot be, without self-annihilation.

Pausing at the table where he sits playing with his last cigarette in the fateful moments before ignition, a woman looks at him sadly from across the drink wavering a few inches below her over-painted mouth.

"What is the exact number of all the geese that have never been in this room," her eyes seem to ask him from across the table.

Awash in the virtue of repetition.

He spent so long trying to become someone else that when he finally became that person he was ready to go back to being the person he had been before.

What is the point of words that will not put us in a precarious position?

How do you build an angel that will not fall?

The paradox of partially offered couscous.

Socrates is a model of the higher life, but it is still life lived as a human being.

The miracle of passion is that no matter how many times it possesses us we are certain that this time it will last.

It is to the extent that each of them resembles a plant, each bloom displaying a rolling tendency, awful, but potent, like saturated fruit, that they are looking so skeptically at the milk.

The magical moment of love's passing passion where they gather together books and memories.

So much for the poetics of desperation.

"What is it that trails red across the floor behind the economy of our kitchen appliances?" he asks.

Her thoughts which are all a part of that great fragment, the truth, the work of art rendered in words which pull feebly at the edges.

Every morning the igneous struggle with the sheets around their ankles seals the external world in its pages.

The pornography of considering what has just been written down.

Underlying the surface of the work is the collective awareness of ourselves as 60% water, and thus susceptible to the slow evaporation occasioned by over-exposure to unmediated language.

Some holes are bigger than the things they're in.

How exquisite for the writer to discover that the project's very essence is captured in a repetitive quality which, due to its source in its multiple beginnings, must forever escape the reader, except perhaps as a residual tedium, because such writing is done for the sake of what its act will expose, rather than what it will communicate.

The fragment as autobiography.

The rain was not to disturb his walk.

He could feel his own body slipping away from him and he thought, "this must be what they call aging."

The sentence felt stilted and lay conspicuously ignored on the table between them.

He considered ethics a technology of self-transformation.

How is the question of whether or not something is art different from the question of whether or not it is good art?

"Who was it that was trying to write a history of the present?"

she asks.

With the classic change upon us.

A music not intended to facilitate orgasm or induce nostalgia.

A selection of offerings from *The Academy of Lists.*

Along the edges of her room the pictures came loose and seemed so helpless.

Murky with lunar gloom.

Corpses of sliced bread grow stiff in the toaster.

Their car in fragments scattered across the sky.

"The only method is to be very intelligent," she says.

She would like to have gone on rewriting Burton's *Anatomy of Melancholy* until all vestiges of her own style had finally been effaced.

Crystal bowls full of artificial fruit, cow's eyes pious in the candlelight, beer bottles popped open.

Nothing more than the accumulation of regret emptying its dregs into the bowl of his desires.

Inured to the tangibility of form, he had to admit he felt fine under the table.

"If you cease to offer them any discernible growth, they will say you are retarded," she warns him.

With violently agitated wrists always close to the jagged edge of the crater.

He accumulates books as if they were fetishes, objects imbued with a power far beyond him, a power perhaps beyond even that of reading.

Passing sentences.

He feels the water lapping at his ankles, tugging him towards a somber absurdity.

Fumbling with their mugs, spoons, sugar packets, and plastic containers of creamer, they find they have as little to say to each other now as when they began.

He recalls the swell of her breasts under her sweater the first day he saw her coming out of the elevator.

And there is the earnest young professor, shielding his erection behind a leather-bound copy of Baudelaire, the pages still uncut except for at "Les Chats," "Le Balcon," "Lesbos," and "Correspondances."

The sun rose larger than a second chance, pouring its coiled light on the scattered bodies of Dutch tulips.

A mortal beam propped against a door of light.

The interrogation of adjectives.

Not an ounce of flesh but that it spends its time upon these scales.

Material objects might include a skeleton, an obstacle to understanding, the door handle, or his pale face in its melancholy.

The Poet stood in the doorway, framed in the headlights of a car stalled in the flowerbed.

Moving through the empty rooms she hears no sound save slaughtered sonnets seeking titles.

The furniture in the room was arranged with an eye to the future.

His palms itched with the desire to touch the skin of her neck.

She feels how there are only a few words left.

What is the metrical line of any given desire?

His tongue in instigation of further contact.

Why must you, as if by virtue of your beauty alone, seek such solaces as those provided by annihilation?

Poetry is simply for the enrichment of living and nothing else.

"I no longer understand," she confesses, "your vocabulary of substance."

He is trying to forget the promise he made himself not to remember.

Writing is a prayer that does not ask for anything.

He was reassured by the line numbering, which seemed to be related to the standard concordances.

She considers the temporal organization of dust a matter of getting the facts right.

He was gradually moving away from the kind of surprises usually associated with the unknown.

Pleasure is the last resort of the hopeless, and the first hope of the rest of us.

Not *philosophy*, but *erossophy*.

He wants an endless repetition of the future to compose his past.

"I want another chance," she says, without specifying at what.

As if time could be an endless unfolding of moments in the present rather than a glancing backwards for what is yet to come.

These thoughts, the groping hand, the misaligned desire of his flesh for hers, words that leak with ill-concealed longing from inadequate lips: what's not forbidden in such clumsy morass?

"Don't," she says; leaving him wondering what it is she has forbidden.

Cartesian inquisitions.

The purpose of poetry is to contribute to the confusion necessary for the essential vibrancy of life.

She embraces the promise of some truth behind his empty gestures.

"I'm not cut out for this," he said, leaving the bloody remains on the table behind him.

Her diaphanous shoes make their way down the hospital

corridor.

I caught this morning sein Blick ist von vorüber gehen the roller of big cigars, la vierge, la vivace, et la belle summer's day, more lovely and more mignon allons voir si über allen Gipfeln ist ruh.

A uniform adds dignity to the act of waiting.

How love stories are told these days as accidental events occurring between the pages of someone else's novel.

She trusts his on-going struggle with honesty to at last reveal the depths of his self-deception.

Isn't it bad enough that Socrates, the Buddha, and Christ never wrote anything, without there being any mention of them ever having read a single book either?

Does she seek a liberation from form without sacrificing the freedom inherent in constraint?

The balancing act.

If it were the case (*ipso facto, quid ergo sum, cumulatus inferatus*) that such contemplation of his past yielded answers for use in the present-progressive (a successful transfer of tenses rendering verbs trans-temporal and of use in a variety of time zones) would he be poised any better for the uncertainties of the future?

He transformed his feelings into words, and in so transforming ceased to feel and wondered, was it worth it?

Ceased to see as through a scrim the hazy world beneath him. The days will pass, and the man like a cat sits on the porch drifting in and out of states of dubious consciousness.

Massive bedlam provides an antidote for that beast without its head.

Such was the power of the sentence that not even the governor could repeal it.

Who would win in a fight, the animals from the circus or the animals from the zoo?

Quickly, the train's motion came to a halt as its momentum was transferred to the flying herd of cattle on the tracks around it.

This was the gentle work of remonstrance at its best.

No horses for those wet cowboys.

Take the calm for what it is.

Porcelain.

She placed her faith in the countless strategies for replacing adjectives with pronouns.

The fillet came back to him.

Poetry is for making life disturbing, surprising, uncomfortable and odd.

Not to comfort the afflicted, but to afflict the comfortable.

Etc.

There is far less learning necessary for wisdom then the learned are willing to admit, but we know how to pursue knowledge, and its acquisition is interminable (and therefore comforting), whereas the paths by which we pursue wisdom are difficult to discover and harder still to follow, and though equally interminable, this quality of unknowablity makes them more daunting and more doubtful.

How are numbers like a liquid?

Erudite suitcase full of dirty laundry no one wants to wash, much less wear.

He could lean his weight into the back of the unsteady chair behind the heavy desk and enjoy the contrived sensation of uncertainty.

Great men are more often the creations of literature then of history—except of course in so far as history is also the creation of literature.

Do concepts such as honesty or depth or perception or nobility or truth still freight their weight in lands like these?

Hamlet's undiscovered country has a solace of its own, a promise of more to come in the act of discovery, where there would be no books to guide him, no more words words words by which to chart his progress.

Just because you can drink out of a bathtub doesn't mean it's a cup.

If it is not a deeper exposure to people, but an escape from them, which we seek to attain in literature, then because a novel inevitably brings the reader into yet further contact with other human beings (even if they are only fictional characters) the goal of literature can more readily be attained in poetry, insofar as it reflects a desire to be free of people.

We live much longer when we live alone, if only because time passes so much slower.

Love is a hole waiting to be filled with human suffering.

In the shadow of ruined dreams she bends down to pluck futilely at her shoelace, waiting at the bottom of the staircase for an endless descent.

Galled at the suggestion that it was created expressly not to work.

For the first time in months they reached out to each other, thinking in unison that perhaps here at last was a person who had the ability to change things simply through the application of language.

Her fingers trace a dull grey path through the dust of what had once been his mind.

As if he were some timeless being, grown old in the observation of other people's lives rather than in the living of his own.

The body can only sustain one sign, however immutable.

Sutured onto the next thing to come along, the touch remains ambiguous.

The writer grants me the logic of my desire and my grief.

At what cost then expression?

Leaves brown and brittle, summer again, the time of refusal.

A place of sounds they've grown accustomed to.

Precepts for poets: Strive to expose the whole world to itself.

Picnicking at a table scarred by switchblades wielded in the evocation of sacred letters.

Their bodies abided by a hollow rhyme scheme, a hectic cascade of syllables.

The World's Sad Retention

His eyes barely see these days and what they do see his mind rejects.

They say that at the moment before death your whole life flashes before your eyes, but how do you know that it is your life and not someone else's?

It is always history, we find, somewhat to our dismay, which seems to herald the abatement of our desires.

There are at least two ways of not knowing, and she knows both of them.

The sun like a door opens onto a room all its own: the stranglehold of daylight.

"When it breaks, you live with the pieces until you learn to live without it," she says.

He was so depressed by its ugliness and meanness that he felt a loathing even for the mirror that revealed it to him.

The revolutions, moth-like, call out to her.

He was beginning to feel like an illiterate knight who has slain the Dragon only to find out that its entire hoard of treasure consists in an old edition of the OED and the maiden he has rescued is a transvestite.

The reader gains a piece of the present because the writer must sacrifice the past and profane the future in order to capture a moment which in turn will be bestowed on language.

Her kisses seemed without yearning.

Flesh marred by the slash of time.

Too late do the innocent run for cover.

Their relationship a literary game of Risk in which he is no more than an already vanquished continent.

I don't expect anything more from life than a succession of sheets of paper to blacken with ink, writes Flaubert.

"It was a problem of prepositions," he explains to the patient bartender: "I wanted to turn her on, she wanted to turn me down."

Isn't any book worth writing worth writing more than once?

Slowly he's learning to behave; he doesn't scream anymore when he sees a pretty girl—at least not out loud.

She listens for a voice that is familiar because it speaks to her of a world that she does not know, has never known, but which nevertheless strikes her as perfectly logical and even recognizable.

The Sea-Goat drinks the moon.

"What kind of strategic articulation do you have available to you in the arena of polymorphic silences?" she asks.

The luminous spaces tamed by their imagination seek records of their progress in the curves and swells of joints and muscles.

The form of narrative as one-way street.

If not poetry itself, at least an act preparatory to such an event.

Her pronouns float in defiant independence from any obviously signified person, place, or thing.

This is not parataxis gone mad because her sentences are related—they just aren't sequential.

Another version of the problem of appropriation.

Qu'est que c'est un livre, finalmente?

Was heisst lessen?

"We're no longer interested in knowledge; we just sort of navigate through the tepid waters of reference."

Air is metal.

They seek the means of returning to wonder (the means of reintroducing prayer into a secular life).

Reeling in nocturnal gyrations she opens her eyes: was it all a dream? a visit to that volcano that occupies her mind?

Sawing away, lost in their music, until the falling dew untuned their strings.

He, like Swann, *had prepared himself for every possibility,* only to discover that *reality must therefore be something that bears no relation to possibilities*.

How thin their lives, in mutual exclusion of each other, had grown.

He doesn't want to change his life, just the person living it.

If to write is to desire, then to read is to desire desire.

She was tired of hearing only pieces of music, from now on she wanted the whole thing.

They confer on plans to hide Nature from her makers.

How we bow before the decaying calendar of our youth.

All part of the narrative illusion.

"What if Kant had been at the Alamo?" she asks.

On the way home their shadows prick the skin of the moon.

Integrating the best-wished-for moments of their lives into easily transmittable sequences of single tone beeps.

"I'm all right for the time being, but later some sort of attention will be required if I'm to be expected to continue functioning normally," he suggests.

Versions of betrayal.

The discharge of meaning.

"Without rejection there is no form," she says.

Does thought have primacy over language? and how can we be sure, confined to thinking even this question in the words which allow us to frame it?

The text exists only as a resonance chamber in which the reader is free to vibrate.

By these confused lines the inventive genius is excited to new exertions.

Music is the saving enigma.

They were other people's words only until she recognized them as, in some unprecedented way, hers all along, and hers with an exclusive creativity that was the very soul of discretion.

She tried to make him believe in the symphonies of color.

He spent weeks in the waiting room at the wrong hospital.

1001 Musical Etudes for Oleg

He imagined that by comparing the minute differences in weight between a blank computer disc and a full one with the differences between a blank cassette tape and a recorded one, he would eventually be able to discover whether information weighed more or less than music.

Writing silences.

What writing condemns her to.

His naked body exposed to ridicule.

The gradual decay of volition.

The whole thing threatens to fall apart, precisely why one might find it beautiful.

There is so much description, but hardly anything to describe.

The eyes and the hand meet in brief temporal union, trying to decide on the body's optional location in space (but it only lasts a few seconds, before things and ideas collapse back into the oblivion of sleep) while thin beams of light trickle in around the window curtain, bearing proof of an external world.

Her mind hovers above a sea of familiar objects which linger just below her grasp, fingers occasionally grazing the surface of the water in an attempt to touch some part of her past.

It doesn't take much to not be enough, which seems like little enough consolation until she's had time to think about it.

"You can only ever run away from yourself," the bartender translates for the rest of them.

Theirs was a season when lovers and writers found an altering speech for altering things.

You can write the word 'door,' but it will not close; return later to find it open on the page before you.

Memories of the Future: an old game they played as children.

Close scrutiny of her work revealed the incredible fact that everything she had written over the last 20 years was in fact no more than an enormous yet finite variation of the ordering, spacing and punctuation of 26 different letters; this stunning revelation, by one of the foremost literary critics of the day, has sent students and scholars alike scurrying back to her work with a newfound appreciation for the formalistic innovation and rigorous methodology of this opus.

Scattered around her feet are the fragments of a language left broken after their last encounter, but she does not know how to respond to his open hostility towards this language, a sort of venomous response to the verbal quality reflected in the sharp edges of the world which has him surrounded.

Although so much is left to chance, he finds uses for things he picks up along the way.

What sort of observations do we expect to find in poetry?

"Why are our thoughts less subject to change than our feelings?" he wonders.

Desire betrays the imagination as it moves forward in time, and imagination defies desire as it moves backwards.

"Certain books and diseases you keep forever," she points out.

"When only desires distinguish us, it is only a matter of time before we are all the same."

How can these daily spinnings seem so insignificant, these bus rides and morning strolls past shops and cafés, these varied waitings, for her paper, her coffee, her turn in line, all of this so singularly unmomentous yet adding up to such disturbing totals?

As they drink the afternoon into a soothing oblivion she shares with him little torn off fragments of her past.

It occurs to him that by starting at the end he would at least spare himself the struggle of not knowing how to finish.

The birds that fall from the sky.

He measures by turn with expectation and by turn with imagination the possible uses of these encountered objects.

His life often felt like the creation of someone else's fantasies conceived on a night of heartburn and undigested cabbage swallowed by the swan of guilty dreams.

Sometimes there is the feeling that every word is a gift, inevitably along with the fear that no one else will ever receive it, that sharing will prove impossible.

The reader turns to the book with expectations and demands, yet brought to the work through these needs, he becomes in turn an object: an object of his own desire.

Perhaps it is the incongruity of the two sides of this equation, the triviality of it all on one side and the fact of her life looming on the other.

"When you frame the frame then what is the picture?" she asks.

Does gnosis flee before him?

No reason to sully one's mind with an act of creation beyond what is suggested by the processes of selection and organization.

He sought for meaning in some special corner of the too-sizable and inchoate pool of information.

They often found themselves equidistant from a variety of possible solutions none of which proved adequate to the exigencies of the situation.

No wonder the abundance left them staring at one another's shoes in vague amazement.

There was a moment before the light started to fade.

The words move around him, circling stealthily as if on green claws through a lush marsh.

Nothing to support her through the interminable loneliness of being herself, day after day.

The mind flows remorselessly.

Her desire wasting his breath before he can catch either, he is carried away and left alone and broken on the shores of his expectations.

Something suggestive in their proximity.

Her body is a wire he has strung between two infinitely distant points.

Footsteps gamble against the solidity of wavering sidewalks sickly pink under solar abuse while hands seek the cool knobs and latches of downtown bars and taverns, the company of grey men in plaid with bottles set before them.

Bit by bit he disassembles her life in one place and reassembles it here in his imagination.

The same thoughts keep resurfacing, turning up like a bad erection that no body will take off his hands.

The miracle that love can grow in such demented conditions is ambiguous—does it attest to the hopefulness of our condition, or to the hopelessness of love?

Poetry begins disappearing from culture because nobody on TV reads it.

Getting off the bus on his way to work he catches a glimpse of a beautiful woman, her image scoring the smooth surface of his morning calm.

Lost among the hallways and galleries of the imaginary magical Museum of the Mind.

She was struck by the depths of longing in so many of us.

There is a silence around the edges that seems to hold them, for a brief moment, in the cusp of its pursed lips.

Roar clip thin raiment of royal blood clothing a colony of rejects.

He felt calm contemplating his own lack.

A smell on the wind reminds her of the poem that caused so much trouble with the neighbors.

How long can he bend his assent to the claim that the mathematical imagination captures the object just as it is?

She reached for his hand across the table and he thought for a moment that she was going to say something; he tried to imagine the words she would use in speaking and he tried to imagine her reasons for remaining silent, and when he reached for the book he had just closed, still lying on the table in front of them, she placed one long thin finger across his lips.

"I confess phenomena concern me."

Concealed in Minerva's tower, minds do not rest satisfied in partial conjunction.

When he notices her writing in a notebook he takes the liberty of informing her that it is primarily due to the inability of so many humans to hear accurately or speak clearly that we owe the rich diversity of languages: "the deaf and inarticulate have done more for the possibilities of poetry than the most polished wordsmith," he says.

She moves off slowly, without waiting for the bus to arrive, leaving him the bench like some surrendered territory of an unspoken war.

What she could not escape she was determined to run all the more quickly toward.

Self-escape is difficult when you constitute your sole means of transportation.

She recalls the moment when epic became collage and tragedy became détournement, when comedy became bricolage and inspiration gave way to plagiarism.

Her imagination would have to create not only the poem, but also the only audience who would ever read it.

Alone in his cell he spent hours staring at the holes in his socks.

Stirred from his reverie, he began running when a host of angry suffixes threatened to crowd him off the page, keeping his distance from the declining verbs and modifying pronouns (declensions were deadly in a climate such as this—a virtual frozen tundra of tendentious conjugations); he did not stop until he could no longer hear their footsteps behind him.

At that moment she would remember the night they met and recall the long, improbable series of events that had led (in hindsight with a seemingly inexorable finality) to this solitary moment on the balcony.

He is plagued by a desire so familiar it's like cutting into the mirror while shaving.

As a bird whirling overhead upsets the delicate balance between fantasy and the price of rice so too do the fish that swim from your mouth to mine upset my heart.

Together each is what the other only dreams of denying.

In a moment alone, to witness the unfolding.

When he closed the book on the table before him he felt as if he had come to the end of something other than his reading.

In other words, the Dragon is his project, and his project traces for him the outlines of his hopes and ambitions, its sweep as wide as the wings of the elusive creature itself.

The constituents of form.

Surgical experimentation.

She had a dream about this in which he walked around in the shape of a metal toothbrush.

"Lagoons are among the most interesting bodies of water," she says.

His solitude was an island that gave the impression of being a peninsula that had broke off just in the nick of time.

In the compilation of sentences she sought solace for the world's betrayal of those early expectations.

A lazy terror.

Those heavy globes of flesh around which so much of the world's anxiety and desire has stormed and raged.

He awoke to find himself in bed with the past.

Her thoughts took on a three-dimensional quality.

We assimilate certain values only to be rejected by them.

There was a geological coercion to this portrait of his dilapidation.

A drunk at the end of the bar is going on about his ex-wife, "I wish I could have known and felt then the things I know and feel now without having had to leave her in order to know them and feel them; but of course that's impossible, since only the experience of leaving her has taught me these things–taught them to me now that the knowing and the feeling are no longer of any use."

As if by way of comfort, the bartender suggests that while distant happiness intensifies present misery, distant misery is simply inexplicable.

He feared the Word crouching like a thick-lipped god, hugging the underbelly, fishing the depths and the shallows looking for carp and carnage.

Splinters of sense.

Spilled on the floor only to be devoured by the ants.

Nothing but distance was moved.

He has for some time reflected on the differences between poetry and fiction: poetry the constantly deferred promise of literature, fiction its inadequate but delightful fulfillment.

Like mushrooms on a damp log, shunned by cats lurking in the dark.

There is a progress to this fair that rolls on wooden wheels across essential days, capricious carnival of whim that shakes at his fancy.

Something familiar about the impossible.

Earlier in life he had swaggered on the very verge of verve; now he barely trickles, the sidewalk an ominous runway.

Measured great by aspiration, felled by faulty ambition.

She lived large upon the miracle of appropriation, fish sticks and candy bars enough to sustain the rest of her.

Every time the doors slid open he expected to see a corpse on the elevator floor, but that didn't keep him from pushing the button.

What had happened to her ambition to write a work in which every word was indispensable?

They sought protection from the letter 5.

He grew impatient with those who stopped to ask where he would stand when the countdown began.

The wave of an effortless flow of language washing over her.

Even the most flexible medium, she has learned over the course of many false starts, premature finishes, and unpleasant middles, must pay some concession to reality.

Imagining the possibility of a 27 letter alphabet.

Turmoil and macerate, massacres, meteors, plagues, spectrums, methodical manner, prodigies, apparitions within reach, wishes, actions, edicts made apparently scant, proclamations by actual measurement, volumes of all sorts.

An unknown habit satisfied with each other's language.

Which passion was made whole by synthesis.

A nascent state found busily in toys.

These activities are not part of the boundaries of his being.

"Visit heuristic Amsterdam," the billboard said.

He was at a loss to explain the teeth marks that appeared on various pages throughout the book.

Someone at the party was explaining to her why the only objectivity is subjectivity in such a way as to make it sound like an attempt to get her clothes off.

He loved the desert because it did not dissimulate its solitude behind crowds the way the City did.

She has come to realize that there are only two things essential to writing: language and thought.

The accumulation of know.

Spaces that deny their antecedent.

When did someone first doubt the claim that language is a sign of thought but not itself the act of thinking?

She spoke with such terseness as would drive a splinter into the flesh of language.

Too many conversations.

Suddenly they pose together in the nude.

All these people wanted to be present while history was being made into something worthwhile.

With holy water slowly drying on the bridge of his nose.

The Name does not cross her lips; it is fragmented into practices . . .

Rings but not fingers are found in ancient tombs.

Then she realized that there is one additional thing also essential to writing: the power to combine them.

He laid waiting for her with great stillness, his body stretched across centuries, pressed against the cold ground.

Talons of milk crossed like bones.

Extirpated spider, unlock your word-hoard.

Gradually she lost her sensitivity to the nuance between finding a place for everything and finding everything's place.

"Its only words running down the drain," she points out, and peering into the black vertical tunnel he hears a sucking noise that suggests that she knows what she's talking about.

But he is not holding his hands out to her so much as keeping them clear of his own body.

As if awareness were a place they sought to occupy.

"What has happened to the courage of appetite?" she asks.

You tremble in the distance of a street laughing at your progress while curling up to meet your falling feet, empty save for the combs and pins and magazines holding down the earth.

Looking at his upturned palms, the fingers curling like undulating sea anemone, she is tempted to pluck at these wavering strands before the water washes them away once and for all.

As she puts the final sentence down on the page, even before the ink has been allowed to dry, she holds the page over the candle and watches her words burn away.

Listening to the buildings grow up from the cement like staggering roses behind which she hides the contours of their mutual limitations.

The utopia of construction.

For centuries we have been seduced by our own nightmares which occupy a realm half in our imagination, half in nature, and wholly in our desire to peer within the inexhaustible diversity of beings and things.

All he has ever wanted was something to get him out of bed in the morning and something to keep him up late at night.

Another vision of a tiresome paradise.

The mind, he thinks, is not something under his control, nor, strictly speaking, is he under its.

The impossible infinity of writing as a response to the infinite desire of the reader?

Until they reach that elusive moment of having been forgotten by the weather.

"Life is work and sex: forms of creation," she suggests, which he calls lush thinking.

Subsidiary to the scenes of tragedy.

There is no overthrowing of our mental habits without a mind to throw them.

Every sound rings true because there is no falsehood in this proliferation of versions.

Square-bodied people in search of slaves find the corpses of their masters.

The door closed with a trembling finality.

A similar combination of words has been seen several times before.

This led him to call the ringing in his ears a performance of the "two sides to every currency" phenomena.

There are some things allowed the poet which bankers should not get away with.

Some wonderful taxonomy.

Eyes ache to produce a body in the universal system of his own rough approximation.

Symbolism a cloak of ignorance.

On the other hand, there are some expressions ("my heart sings," "the wings of night," "the moon's remorse") that poets should avoid, even if they sound refreshing coming from the plumber as he wiggles around under your kitchen sink.

Compositions and methods are both lengths.

Language is no excuse.

Giants of old cannot be true.

It will, at times, pause and step outside itself as if in an effort to describe itself.

Pleasure is a complex polyhedron.

He had exorcised pornography from his eyeballs, but lust still seethed in his soul.

Bent to the sway of wanting.

Not to live in a world where axiology is anatomy.

He called her eyes *these ships cutting with their prows his thoughts from their anchor*.

"Why would a philosopher fight for the 'probable impossible' over the 'possible improbable'?"

Her legs folded beneath her shaking body and the holes running in and out of her remaining light.

Writing is the result of abolishing or defying thought, in stanching an excessive flow, in control, but not in surrender, for if the writer were to surrender it is the reader who would be captured.

"I write slowly," she says, "because the goal is not to have written something, but to observe how the act of writing operates upon my soul."

Even the most embarrassing sentence will at least be over soon.

It seems that with time language had grown into something cumbersome that blocked their view of one another.

Bilateral yawn.

At that time, real sound existed.

Swirled around by the eye of that desperation, afraid of the stillness that should be the end of all frantic compulsion.

You check her outlines.

A modicum of desire, misdirected.

She removed his hand from her waist before he was able to locate the dress's zipper.

How unlike his thoughts are to those birds accustomed to swooping.

Their grammar flowed at even pace.

Deep brown body and creamy skin beyond the belief of touch.

The lost feeling they occasionally share serves to locate them at the interstices of an inflexible material web.

A frustrating position: hard work is the easy part, if only one can determine precisely what work needs to be done.

Extracting the fragments of bone.

The immediate fruit of their efforts was an infinite list of finite things.

We are concerned with the saving of our souls, whether we believe in them or not.

A poem is a combination of words that we cannot imagine until we are faced with them, after which we cannot imagine the world without them.

According to Aristotle's *De Anima, The soul is a place of forms.*

Living is the art of asking.

Together they share the task of learning to enjoy hunger as a physical pleasure.

She was in one of those moods in which she sought to apply definitions to herself, and then rejected each definition as soon as she understood what it meant.

Like a poem the sound of the falling body rang out in the room below.

Yet still they do not grasp.

His fascination with her desire to rewrite the *Cantos* stemmed from their shared inability to abandon the project of Modernism.

After several hours of waiting, she realized with horror that the arms of the clock on the wall were stationary, but that the face itself was gradually rotating.

A little fresh position finished overslept.

How unfortunate to discover that the sun is the analog of pain.

His hopes which were to be carried on the back of a camel through imaginary deserts for a hundred years.

Far off they can see solitary gusts of wind spelling out their confusion.

The end came in winter.

The depths of an animal's consciousness buried deep within her.

His fascination with Modernism stemmed from his desire to understand the compelling influence of certain books that no one wanted to read.

"I don't want to write novels because I don't want to create people; I have enough trouble with the real people in my life without making up new ones to haunt my imagination, where I probably do too much of my living as it is."

Sometimes he feels that earnest readers are like plumbers in a world without toilets: masters of an arcane realm of knowledge that is no longer useful or even comprehensible to anyone else.

She knows that what one spends a lifetime doing will eventually become that lifetime.

He persists in hauling around behind him a collection of objects that he thinks will make him who he is, and he continues encouraging others in the same mistake until it is hardly even considered a mistake any more.

Art too is a way to hide.

Suspended from the gleaming steal girders running along the roof of her mouth, hanging on every word.

The problem with too many writers is that they want to show to the reader what they fail to see themselves.

She invokes their names like magic spells.

How does the sentence fulfill its duty to communication through strategies of betrayal?

Caught up in the immaculate apperception of her experience, with the cool demeanor of a hard boiled egg left naked on the counter of a diner for several days, she at length felt inclined to expose herself to the inclement atmosphere of sharing which the others in the group perpetuated.

He clung to fragments of the past as a shabby means of holding together the tattered pieces of the present.

An infinite number of one or two things desirous of being known.

What can a word do to the mind?

Those little cereal boxes were a memory from a childhood she watched on TV while growing up.

He is waiting patiently to hear back on an NEA grant application he has submitted for a project which involves replacing the Bibles in hotel rooms with copies of Joyce's *Ulysses*.

As usual, there were determining factors beyond their control.

They share a fleeting moment of honest exposure before the innocent flower becomes the forbidden fruit.

His notion of reality is not characterized by idealism so much as by a yearning for beauty marked by a failure to communicate.

The gradual accumulation of an impression.

That she might know that what she heard was a true movement of desire's beating wing.

Each stirred thoughtfully their cups.

She has not yet convinced herself that she has nothing to prove to anybody.

From a pocket of his overcoat he takes out a small book bound in red leather.

They smile and reach simultaneously for the bowl of plastic fruit on the table between them.

The total structure of our soul and body consists of musical harmony.

To master some small corner of a pathetic universe and there lie quietly and unassuming.

Meanwhile, the toast stands abandoned in the toaster, waiting stiff and erect for absent fingers and rancid butter.

Undisturbed by atmospheric discrepancies, he suffers a benign influence of the mind which gives him a hankering for impossible journeys through the realms of time.

The sentence, over the course of several hundred pages, had taken on a life of its own.

A voyage whose ends were not right.

Although motion certainly strikes him as important in terms of being essential to achieving a change in place, he is not at all confident about his ability to affirm the existence of these places.

She floats vaguely beneath the surface of a century without waves.

Like a door this simile closes off a room.

He knows that when the door swings open she will rise to meet the figure who enters from the darkness, but he does not know what it will take to become that figure.

One has faith either in miracles of long ago, or in paradises yet to come, or in the present eternally postponed in the name of poetry.

He is concerned with the lack of distance involved in travel.

The words find her waiting, overcome, supine, prone in expectation of their caress, their gaze.

Thought became the subject of his meditations.

Astonished in the darkness.

Riding the bus he sees a woman taking off her sweater and revealing a strip of skin across her lower back, but only for a moment; when it's gone, it's gone: what it leaves behind is worse than what was never there before.

"I would blow myself up if I thought it would change the world, or I would blow up the world if I thought it would change me," she says.

He dares not speak of pleasure.

Starlight flickers across her screensaver.

How does poetry respond to the fact that violence has become society's most marketable commodity?

Words help make life more accessible.

Unrecoverable souls.

The answer glared up at her like fluorescent toads emerging from a contaminated sewer.

Caught up in the language of complicity.

He tried to translate his spiritual quest into an intellectual process in order to stave off feelings of doubt brought on by the uncertainty of inaction.

Days like stubborn gypsies stripped of their colored wagons.

Each image stains his mind dark-blue purple like a bruise; each bruise collects blood under the skin; each skin encounters friction in the act of love; each love aches for the return of its own innocence; each innocence collects blood under the skin; each skin glistens with sweat as in an act of recrimination.

Burning under the rubric of appetite.

He casts a colonial gaze across the thematic organization of her topography of resistance.

Riding the bus her head bobs along like a shock of scarlet seaweed in an ocean of newspapers; she feels as safe here as anywhere, and considers for a moment the possibility that she might never get off.

To arch one's back at pleasure's taunting sneer.

But time is running short; soon a spider-mouthed woman will drag him away from all this, her kiss a blow that leaves him helpless, paralyzed in the space between knowledge and desire.

Grammar is not about rules, but constraints.

At those times when nothing more fearful than symmetry and the memory of Loyola's *Spiritual Exercises* held him together.

A lapse might be more than an opportunity.

It hurts his eyes to look at her, to watch her hands turn the pages of his books.

Same disease, different treatment.

Solidity is more urgent than one imagines.

A voice speaking to her from the void says that soon she will be able to leave this place, although by then there will be nowhere left for her to go.

"A man should not be afraid to include himself in his own index," she says.

Nothing to prove.

He finds himself stepping on the heels of those in front of him while being tread on in turn by those behind.

The deferment was perpetual.

He sees the surface of her face as an unbent branch resting in a glass of water.

They grasp futilely at their receding futures, fingers falling on cut glass tumblers casting shadows on mahogany.

No paradise for lost insurrectionaries.

She stirred in her sleep and he awoke aligned along her back, his penis lay shriveled against her thigh like a worm.

Desire has been displaced, but not for long.

They linger under this shadow still, confined by the space of the specific yet subject to the general's hollow will.

Years of we.

To choose between their lost vicissitudes.

One of those amazing dictionaries in which every entry was a definition for a different word.

They watch each other without admitting it, even to

themselves.

Thinking is.

Seeking the means to chart his progress from isolated self-consciousness to participant in the World Spirit.

Free of ambition but driven by the fear of nonproductivity. Biting her lip as a prognostic device.

Crouched in the folds and angles of imagination, she deploys night in the service of vague monsters.

Their daily motion would appear effortless if not for their struggle against the objects propelling it forward.

She listens again for the sound that ravished the mind.

The idea of reading just for pleasure was such a shock to him that for a moment he could not recall the other reasons why he had for so long pursued the craft.

Searching for some visible sign of her disappointment.

The completion of a final round of interviews before the candidates are systematically eliminated.

Language was the mask behind which he hid from the world.

Throwing Madonna.

As if a sudden movement would threaten the very balance between the trees and sky.

Meanwhile the neglected lips begin to drool.

"Thus I begin to understand sandwiches."

For weeks he felt sad at the thought that we no longer cut the pages of the books we read.

"Perhaps our velocities engender revolutions," she suggests.

From beneath the sheets the words feel so familiar.

There is only the hope that to continue will not run itself down.

Even words would move beyond their points of tolerance.

She was staring through the window without seeing anything.

Does he submit to what he sees, the opposition of this world to all that he protects inside?

He finds her stretched in contemplation naked on the couch, waiting for the microwave to begin transmission.

Since love has so little to do with logic, the forsaken one is forced to spend the rest of his life in the indeterminate space created by two opposing explanations.

Trying to attain a full range of motion across the gulf of his idea, he hesitated long enough to suggest the need for a second chance.

The shoe dropped with that air of finality reserved for significant gestures.

He feels the words moving inside him, like mice in the walls, dodging the nails and bits of plaster.

She had long sought to inhabit one of those rooms described

by Proust as *thickly powdered with the motes of an atmosphere granular, pollinated, edible and devout.*

Crouched among the wilting flowers.

Language and thought, and the ability to combine them—and the time necessary to do so.

The accumulation of no.

Hadn't the decision to remove been the only act of eradication necessary?

A beautiful object is one thing, a beautiful idea another: one skips rocks across the lake of the imagination while the other drowns silently in the shadow of intent; each beats out a local rhythm in a foreign head, and neither is enough to make a poem.

Her gown rattled about her ankles as she floated through dim houses aware of how many of their words, the furniture of this ghostly world, could so easily be dispensed with.

Because he prefers not to admit defeat, his definition of victory remains ever changing, floating between a particular idea of the ineffable and an entelechy of enlightenment.

He had never lost his fascination for those marbles which, alternately translucent and opaque, brilliantly colored and mysteriously shadowed, had captured his childhood imagination more forcefully than the most beautiful and precious gems.

Thus it was not some misguided notion of temporary oblivion, submissive and subject to her control, which would provide her with the grammatical structure that her sentences, aflame with a green light, craved.

It had not yet occurred to him to ask whether there might be degrees of reality, and if so, whether these degrees might be discernible by him.

It was the hope that eventually their memories would outweigh the present that, along with poetry, alcohol and, occasionally, their unique form of sexual intimacy, held them tenuously together.

In her world computers are low moving canines shaped like cylinders.

Old technology grinds slowly in her interim.

He likens the frustration of talking to her with the act of talking to himself in a broken mirror against which he kept slashing his tongue on the shards of glass.

Beholden to the freshly minted God of English, words imprinted across his brow and upon his flesh draped like loose fitting garments upon a newly laid out corpse.

They made love over his dead body.

Another casualty of a history he had lived through but did not survive.

Imaginary homes composed of desire, memory, and remorse, gradually replace the geographic locations of her temporal frame.

When he said "yawning vacuum" she thought he was talking about bored appliances.

Wearing a shirt of tears.

A love without vowels.

Lost below the surface of the waters of forgetfulness.

The words are only a means of temporarily forestalling the inevitable return of desire.

A question about the pigeons.

He feels each sentence, like a layer of flesh around his bones, building him up from the inside out.

In the room a single candle continues to burn while gingerly she fingers the bruises culled from endless cycles of hellos and good-byes and the kisses and movies and food and fucking in between.

She says, "ask yourself what you really want and face the possibility that you've gotten the answer wrong for years, maybe for your entire life."

Every page an abyss.

But what if this is only the same old song and dance about art returning us not to an idealized version of our past, but to the hollow rooms of our future?

A fluid's octave.

The syntax of orbits.

Love made possible by distance, no matter how close we are.

When she feels that emptiness and desperation spreading out from the past and threatening to engulf the present, she takes up her pen.

What takes place outside of history is always a comfort to those who have already given up.

Moving through elaborately constructed mirages of his own imaginings.

Approaching squalor.

If only there were more than the contingency of communication to bind me to this world.

Words which were no longer part of the invocation of wonder.

Pleasure is the simplest and most difficult literary genre because each member of the cast of characters wants to be told in the first person.

Between 'I' and 'You' lies the most desolate grammatical space, the crossing of which leads to 'We' or 'Us', but never for very long; this space reinscribes itself: there is always a 'They' shoveling sand in the desert.

The poem is our modern medium of design, the metropolis of mental life, a factory for the production of uneasy happiness, a machine for modern living that moves for us our joints and limbs and keeps them lubricated.

Plenty of room around the edges, frayed and extending beyond polite boundaries.

In their dreams of a past which does not forgive they wander through a desert of gymnastic apparatus smelling of decayed nightgowns eventually to find themselves sleighing through Russian winter nights between the Churches of Moscow and St. Petersburg orgies.

Fire becomes a small ring with a stone in it.

He knew then why steps, door handles, and shop windows exercised a power of seduction over her.

Power made his suits fit better.

The untutored signifier will be cut up into a series of brief, contiguous fragments.

He lifts his fork in response to her enthusiasm, remarking that sausages, too, are the repositories of so many of life's mysteries.

A weak-kneed moment.

"This is to inform you that the state of my feelings toward you as an affective object has evolved in a markedly positive direction," the note read.

Her work is a fragment of substance occupying a portion of the spaces of books.

Such feelings must have been founded on ephemeral wisps of unexamined minutiae that bore no relation to the other contradictions upon which they based the decisions that reigned over their lives.

"What do you think about the way our eyes focus on the approaching objects of perception?" she asks.

He recalls that Sir Philip Sidney spoke frequently of imitating the inconceivable.

As if a pseudo-sympathy for positivism was enough to make his flailing metal efforts appear more rigorous.

She had a system for beating the system, a simple case of constructing one unique mode of transportation to remove herself from her last recorded position before moving on to the next anticipated condition.

Their executioners, who wrote poetry between sentencing people to the guillotine, were highly educated, cultured people, familiar with the idea of "life in the colonies" as it came to be known during those days when wicker furniture gave off clouds of billowing black smoke as it burned on the porches of plantation houses doused with cane liquor and fanned by the breeze of wide brimmed Panama hats.

Who has not written under (or tried to write out from under) the shadows of Futurism (both Italian and Russian), Dada, Surrealism, Cobra, Bauhaus, Stein, Duchamp, Cage, Situationism, the Oulipo, Fluxus, Language Poetry—in short, under the various shadows of the avant-garde?

Today they look with hope toward the prospect of a world free of natural forces: only the inevitable shakes their confidence.

It is a lot of weight for a page of print and a glass of gin to sway under.

Words held lovingly by the swollen tongue, fingers restlessly playing in matted hair.

When they spoke it was as if their tongues walked on crutches.

Time sucked its last, their bodies hollow straws.

Days without weather.

Blighted talent builds a mansion of rage.

His brain like a wasteland.

Our most difficult moral decisions are not choices between right and wrong, but between two things both of which are right but which are in conflict with one another.

"Love is comic and tragic," she tells him, "tragic in its comedy, and comic in its end."

Falling short of love, they might continue to dance to the imminent rhythms of their lives, and, failing that, there were the movies, donuts, and the ability of sex, booze, poetry, and 11 a.m. breakfasts to hold two people together across that gulf of the combined weight of their past histories, future fears and present insecurities.

"You have to read something, otherwise you'd be reading nothing, and to be reading nothing, how would that protect you from the potential meaninglessness of existence?"

A fortuitous combination of words can result in a perfectly natural sentence.

She wanted to write something about Dragons, about how the sound they make walking through the marshes keeps squishing through her ears.

Suddenly alarmed by the imminence and immanence of the first person, she quickly backed out of the corner she found herself in.

After an absence of several days a residual longing began to appear.

This time rubber silences their gestures.

It was one of those days during the course of which she was able to forget, sometimes for hours at a time, how many years of effort a single line had cost her.

Over glasses of juice on Spanish terraces they weigh the checks and balances: whether 'tis nobler to bear the slings and arrows of outrageous fortune, or abdicate a manifold and duplex life.

Esteemed umpires of taste, the sun sparkles in the liquid, the ice settles in their glasses.

Circling words for elimination, art hung about the walls with careless abandon.

Titillation expedites desire.

Yet he knows that rooms full of French portraits do not a museum make.

On such days her favorite words were ones indicating indecision and reconsideration.

Dismal the defeats they came to call their own.

While heat erupts white empires need toppling.

She could feel reality ominously moving.

As they moved along the silent line arms would occasionally reach out from the dark and grab a cringing figure or a club would fall on the head or shoulders of some cowering victim.

They did not know where to turn within this new form of loneliness.

She sifts through the shoebox on the floor in front of her, words worn smooth, greasy with the thumbing and fingering of others.

Or she holds out for that flexibility of mind necessary to step into the condition of indeterminacy.

Fingering the helpless pen she wonders if she might stumble back upon a writing that neither created a life nor destroyed one, but only postponed the act of living.

The mouths of isolation.

The walls of the passage seemed to be getting narrower.

What kind of invention is the sock?

The poet looks at numbers, colors, laws of nature, music, ideas, planetary gases, hope, physics, the chemistry of fear, money, love, desire, books, images, despair in God, the awful power of smell, horses, law, history, cleaning agents, space—all through words.

But words are all they have with which to bring the imagination down to earth.

Like everything in love, it is all they have, less than they want.

The words are scattered recklessly; dance among them if you dare.

The books, by now, were everywhere; taking over the house, replacing sex, read late into the night, casting shadows across naked shoulders; she catches him in the middle of the night reading by furtive light, his eyes hanging on the last few words on the page like a needle dangling from his arm.

In other words, words have meaning, but where does this meaning come from? from the world itself which the words somehow point to (a kind of correspondence theory of meaning) or from our use of the words, or from some other source altogether?

She writes because she is unhappy, but because writing makes her happy, she has come to be happy in her unhappiness so long as she goes on writing.

As an artist she felt guilty letting all this guilt go to waste, but as a person she felt bad about the fact that the "as an artist" part of her could not exculpate or redeem the "as a person" part of her.

Living in opposition to life's symptoms.

Even so, there were moments during which she felt a sense of creeping desperation, as if her writing were not in fact a means to an end, but rather a means to the end—the end she hastens towards with every passing word.

What is the relation between what we think and the medium (language?) in which we think it?

The mind flows remissly.

In order to deepen her relationship with language upon which, so it seemed to her then and still seems now, all else depends.

It is always and never too late, and at best the work we do is as close as we will get to who we are.

Among the various items in her collection of lists are a number of questions she wishes someone would ask her.

If the mind makes the decision to shut itself down, what makes the decision to turn it back on again?

It was 3:00 a.m. when Elvis' *Love Me Tender* came on the Donut Shoppe's piped-in radio for the third time since he had been sitting there over coffee and cigarettes.

She inured herself against hope by waiting needlessly in lines at post offices, the DMV, banks, and the tax bureau.

What could van Gogh have meant when he wrote, *In the intercourse with women one especially learns so much about art*?

Immunized against a need for information.

He knew already what no one would read; he had anticipated just such a library.

A certain elegant pliancy reigned over the whole.

There is no happiness in poetry; it is not a space we set aside for anything but waiting.

The noon trains ran at night.

Fingers dance over the shadows of still objects on the waiting table.

The acts of restitution seemed endless.

Would continuing, if it were possible, only be worthwhile if the continuation of continuing itself were guaranteed?

The heat reminds him of one of those scenes in a novel in which the detective suddenly realizes he's been betrayed by the girl and tricked into shooting his best friend.

Each sentence a thin yellow line running through a ripe ample button.

She hears the scrape of a dead tree branch on the cracked windowpane and feels the stiff forearm muscle dragging itself across the sheet of paper.

He is sitting under a tree that drops leaves on him from time to time, but there is still enough sun left filtering into this corner of the yard to squint by.

Voices he should have clung to splinter at the sound of locking doors.

Her lips and hair dusty as if a train had just arrived in her sleep and she was looking for someone on board.

Speaking to a pile of books on the table in front of him: "If I was the kind of man who could have believed in God, then I guess I'd have believed, but since I couldn't believe in God, I believed in you instead; I suppose believing was something I needed, no matter in what."

The tree drops another leaf.

"I was always worried about knowing things, and about the way words could keep track of that knowing; I thought she was a part of those words, but she was more."

He looks up expectantly at the sound of footsteps on the gravel, heralding the approach of someone he has never seen before.

His eyes capture desire.

Only an English mind could have conceived of combining hedonism with calculus.

Each universe a word.

The economy of the imagination.

A taste for the extraordinary is characteristic of mediocrity, warns Diderot.

Radiant but resisting forms.

Unruly unison.

This may only be a reproduction, but as he chose to reproduce it, he remains culpable.

For if Socrates posited knowledge as a form of being, epistemology as ontology, then reading, which he saw as a form of knowledge, might also lead to some desired but still unknown state of being.

Day comes edging over the night's slipping grasp as if yesterday had split in two.

A controlled fracture of light.

Arrangement by laceration.

Do we really believe that an epistemological condition might by necessity engender an ontological status?

Only the impossible stretches beyond these limits which they erect in order to approach each other.

Disillusioned librarians desperate to renew their youth.

Such methods naturally object to the flow of things.

In regards to certain positions various combinations have already been eliminated.

Fractured control.

A machine except in purpose.

Days like these don't come around every 24 hours.

He would not mourn lest he recover from this.

Who would have thought that something as simple as writing a sentence would prove to be so persistently difficult?

Two dangers never cease threatening the world: order and disorder.

The serenity of immense design is missing from her life.

However irregular and desultory his methods, there is order in the fragments of his task.

Growing dim against the horizon of expectations.

"Having Dragons appear without heads is good," she reassures him.

Are there Dragons in the wings of the world?

. . . the Dragon, as the radiance of consciousness, changes unfathomably, able to ascend and able to descend, able to be large or small, able to hide or appear; when you face it, you do not see its head; when you follow it you do not see its back . . .

The Dragon is the symbol of envy; it is consumed by envy because it has no venom—an idea altogether consistent with the zoology of the Middle Ages, according to which the Dragon belonged to the third order of serpents, those "whose bite may be fatal even without venom."

And I have been shown a priestess from that land—one of the tribes of the Massylians—who guards the shrine of the Hesperides; for it was she who fed the Dragon and preserved the holy branches upon the tree, sprinkling moist honey and poppy, bringing sleep— she promises to free, with chant and spell, the minds of those she favors but sends anguish into others.

Then did the ground between the two wheels seem to me to open; from the earth, a Dragon emerged; it drove its tail up through the chariot; and like a wasp when it retracts its sting, drawing its venomed tail back to itself, it dragged part of the bottom off, and went its way, undulating.

Dragons battle in the field; their blood is dark yellow.

Destroying the insidious antinomy of form and content.

Fragments of truth torn out of connection.

When do they use 'pleasure' as a verb?

The telephone went unanswered in the other room.

Their fingers found each other beneath the table.

Complicity engendered license.

It is hunger that makes a difference.

He could taste the burnt flavor of coffee on his tongue.

A sandwich stirred her imagination.

If they move through the City, past distant buildings and over buckled concrete and bubbling tar, it is not without a sense of intimacy mediated by the distance between their bodies and the bodies that tremble at their passing.

She listens again for the sounds of ravished mind.

Language was the mask behind which he hid the world.

As he had predicted, they made love over his dead body.

Specifically, language's ability to *imitate the inconceivable.*

The months of insulation.

Things slipped inevitably from uncertainty into habit.

They have come to learn that the process by which we unlearn the essential things we need to know in order to avoid taking things for granted is itself obscure.

The mind long accustomed to wandering elsewhere, through landscapes devoid of objects or nature or even of people beyond what you can make of them.

She has listened with ears perched just beyond the realm of the senses.

No subject except the subject constructed from the outside.

She composes change in search of order.

Her smile sits below the surface of the horizon, waving a red flag in dismal weather.

Identity, as with the tides, seems to come and go.

The daily selection of those objects representing choice in our lives.

She promises him that on that day of being absolutely terrified he will look like he is not afraid at all.

The fog rolled over the cats and sprawled at the foot of the stairs, its gaping maw waiting to swallow their descent.

She seeks wonderful moments of serenity.

Standing under the trembling moon the vampire gave the impression of having other places to be.

She saw ink as her last chance for egress.

He remembers burgers outside on 16th St., watching the traffic and the cops in the already warm spring night and the aimless wandering down familiar video store aisles, later his lips traveling along her stomach to that arbitrary line below which her hands would always stop him, and he remembers the first night they did not, more exciting still for all the times they had before.

Art and science are not opposed, nor are they the same; they are simply modes of understanding.

That the novel is not identical to writing is evident from the fact that in the greatest novel of the modern age Proust discovers that writing becomes possible only *at the end* of the novel (by the time the narrator becomes the author the novel is already over) – in fact, writing begins where the novel ends (and what the real-life author renders in fiction, the fictional author is left to render in reality).

In the mind, one must always leave a door open.

She wanted to get to him before his eyes had a chance to focus.

There are no hard surfaces to the shapes of our aesthetic insurrections.

Thus their sense of self becomes a function of their interpretive strategies.

Had she been freed from the dominion of the text or cast out from its protective sheltering?

"Who will hold us accountable?" she asks.

While he is busy counting her tattoos (one for every year he's been away).

When systems replace thought.

Poetry is an expression of dismay at language's inevitability.

The Continuing Adventures of Their Sentence

He knows a book is not going to change anything, the way a junkie knows he's got a habit, but this knowledge does not extinguish hope, or the desire to pursue it.

The distance between writing a word and thinking a word is so great that in that one instant she loses all the feeling thought provides.

Caught up in the plot of grammar's seduction of vocabulary.

Who would remind them of the danger of confusing pleasure with happiness, or happiness with something worth living for?

We are each of us as much slaves to the ideologies of the cultures we are born into as we are to the mysteries of those we are not.

"The line between loathing and ecstasy depends on what you've become accustomed to," she says.

Poetry as an interrogation of the past in order to make sense out of the present.

The screaming was deafening yet when it stopped they missed the sense of direction it had provided.

She leans forward with her cigarette into the outstretched lighter.

He owed her a debt of structure, the ability to organize his thoughts around a set of images or ideas.

The storm threw a fat child into the street.

"Oh, it's certainly a poem," he assures her, prodding it gently with his toe again in order to make sure.

Having seen only part of New England, memory edits more ruthlessly.

His speech gradually depopulated of the use of universal predicates.

So that no one would crack the code of his elaborate compact with confusion.

As if their lives ran parallel to each other, but intersected in a series of patterns that did not even lie on the grid.

America struck her as a tragic land inhabited by a comic people, a misstaged event.

She opens her mouth in anticipation.

"Do not relax the tension or let go of the rope even for an instant," she says.

Love too has *gone the way of all buttons.*

"What is it that we'd like to know before it's over?" she asks.

How could he gaze at the world with dazed indifference when in any direction some source of torture met his eyes?

Busloads of Victorians unload at crucial points.

His imagination provided her with unmediated access to the history of language.

Not for the feigned of heart.

What was it he wanted? or was the question hard to answer because knowing the answer and getting what he wanted were in fact the same thing?

Political theories are simply the articulations of values: if you do not share the value, you will not support the theory.

But perhaps he didn't really want anything, and what he wanted was not to realize that fact.

Imagine her surprise upon discovering that someone had already written the conversation between Shakespeare's Bottom, Spinoza, and Wittgenstein that she had been imagining all these years.

That sort of thing can put a damper on anyone's creativity.

There are certain chemicals, harmless as liquids, the residues of which become rather fiercely explosive once evaporation takes place.

You realize that secretly you were expecting something more after 40 years of poetry (which may simply be a way of making it easier to accept that actually what you were expecting was something more after 40 years of life).

Final judgment might be indefinitely postponed until the question of value itself is seen in a new light.

Enjamb me not.

He had as last encountered that book that he had always dreamed of discovering, only to find that it was too staggeringly beautiful to tolerate being read.

She has lost thatperfectcontrol of the spacebar that characterized her early writing.

He seems to have gotten lost somewhere in the midst of checking out of his transient existence.

Misplaced signifiers of false intentions.

The proliferation of passion.

The vocation of desire.

"Anyone can write a poem, but how many people actually know how to read one?"

At sea in the process of art.

The wounded man, so recently bereft of love, lies bleeding on the floor of a hotel room that resembles his childhood bedroom as he remembers one by one the books and toys that have disappeared with his innocence; on its back in the shadows the Teddy Bear sprawls like a grasping hand, beckoning or pleading, its legs shoot up like the yearning fingers of Michelangelo's Sistine Chapel.

When true understanding finally comes he is standing outside an all-night BBQ restaurant hoping he will find his keys before someone inside convinces his date that although there is no actually infinite we will always have the pleasures of the potentially infinite.

In a dream she has finally written the poem she always wanted to write, but in doing so it was necessary to destroy the entire universe.

Like toys in search of children.

Bataille knew: *I write, I suppose, out of fear of going mad.*

When the desire returns the words will rise up to meet it.

There were words enough, when it came right down to it.

Sitting around listening to all-weather radio he can see through the open front door behind his right shoulder the sun-lit street and the chrome fender of a pick-up truck and can hear the drone of neighborhood lawnmowers.

Her role models were miniature men and women who kept peeping out of the bushes and laughing at her from behind their hands.

He remembers watching the pale students file into the test

center, clutching their number 2 pencils, nervous eyes pacing across their foreheads.

Vor Freude tanzend, stieß er gegen den Elefanten.

Racing so far back we get ahead of ourselves.

Upon this desperate planet of their need.

Tourists of the fourth world.

She was clearly obsessed with totality (for she sees that de Sade is walking along hand-in-hand with Hegel and they have no interest in slowing down for her whatsoever).

As one lie gave way under the eventually undeniable weight of truth another was already on the rise—each one providing him with the fulcrum necessary to lift himself up to the next before the previous one collapsed under the onerous burden required to sustain it.

She counted on saving herself at the last minute with a calculated packaging of culture's exoticism as a cunning response to the market's demands.

The poem began, "In seeking the limits of what we are allowed to say . . ." and was accompanied by incredibly vivid images of the dismantling of the universe.

If she could write two words for every one he read, then eventually, hydra-like, she was bound to outstrip even his most extravagant ambitions.

We design our own space constraints.

The statement *the cat is on the mat* filled him with an

epistemological dread matched only by the referential terror it conjured up.

We cannot prey on what is beautiful.

His passport to eternity void of stamps.

Paralytic against the horizon of her eagerness.

Living just short of the threshold of possibility.

A verb that fits between the worlds' jointed countenance.

It was not the form of an idea but its scope that held his interest.

It is the work behind an instant decision that gives it depth.

The act of deletion, of erasure, a positive cipher.

Every turn a source.

An oasis behind every dune.

The opulent curves of self-doubt.

Harboring a fugitive suspicion.

The crucifix of certain emotional vectors.

The poem is not in any ordinary sense *about* its subject; it is an attempt to be "the thing itself."

To rebuild the tower of Babel from a five foot shelf of books and perch there precariously waiting for the hand of God to bring it all tumbling down.

Where do they go, those words you delete from your computer screen when you no longer want them?

And how was I to ever cross the wavering shimmering wiggling line dividing my hand from your body?

Nor is his relation to the world compensated for by an infinitude of inconceivable contraction, an adventure of categories into the vortex sought.

A smile sliced like a mile-long thumb from the hand of a green grocer.

Disremembering dismembering disremembering.

He smiles at the torn flesh around her eyes.

No aesthetic refraction.

Just how far would his dislike of magazines take him?

What Kierkegaard must have meant when he spoke of *an atom in the eternal possibility that was his soul*.

When just keeping up feels like falling behind.

Desire is the world's imposition upon our failed attempts at self-containment.

The text and the reader enter a complex web of interrelationships that includes the author, history, society, and myriad other social, ethical, and aesthetic forces, all of which serve to raise the question: who then, in this web, is the spider?

Art has failed when it becomes part of the shell we place around something we don't care to see.

At which time he developed no less of an attachment to something that makes a squeaky noise when it moves in the dark.

Soliloquies in hell amidst the voices of angels.

And should love elude you even here?

Days go by and the result is generalities that cut like particulars.

Although the planets conspire, he keeps coming back to landscapes.

A version of the American Dream no one had woken up from in time to have.

Reading about Kerouac getting drunk is not the same as getting drunk, and getting drunk is not the same as finding what she's after.

The feeling of incompleteness is absolutely necessary, how could one go on without it (even (especially?) if going on consists entirely of the effort to complete this incompletion)?

One needs one's lack as a complement to one's abundance and it is difficult to imagine how we might find any value in one without the other.

Comforted by his exposure to an expanding frontier of ignorance.

What they catch with the skillfulness of words falls far short of what they aim at, falling like a clean shirt off the line onto the trampled grass and mud.

Nor are they any closer now, having covered so much ground, than they were at a much earlier, but equally impotent stage of ignorance and uncertainty.

Birds swoop low as if to distribute greetings while in a room with white shutters someone goes blind while getting into bed.

And yet philosophy is no less noble for the impossibility of its ambitions.

Production secreted through the fingertips from a source more private than the body.

Heaps of language littered about in piles along the railroad tracks.

The stars lay within a wheel and spun at terrific speed.

He remembers the pleasure of vodka and Yoo-Hoo on hot afternoons.

The swell of her.

Although the order was important, this is not to say that there did not exist other orders which might be equally so, so that in a sense the order was not important, or only arbitrarily so, however deliberate its original arrangement.

Her third novel was a 600 page reflection on half an hour spent sitting on the couch in her living room—she can't even remember the first two.

He knows that we have been trained to think of something called "the limits of language," but does calling something this call it into being?

Outside of language, whatever our thoughts are doing has no name.

She raises her arms to enhance the horizon.

The wheel moved along the perimeter of an enormous square fastened firmly to the disc.

Dreaming lazily of a broom carrying the day for the allies.

The poem is an act of the mind.

Fascinated by the motion of her hands stroking opinions.

"Information is not the answer," he reassures himself.

How many years had she wasted seeking proof of an external world rather than evidence of an internal one?

Not the will to try, but the faith to continue.

For many years it was enough to say that reading was simply one of the ways of enlarging your world, but what happens when you begin demanding something else from books?

There's little point in asking for faith, since faith is precisely that which allows us to ask for things in the first place.

If this is all there is it will have to be enough; for that matter, it will have to be enough even if it isn't all there is.

Two people—not necessarily the poet and the reader—are brought together through language: this is the miracle of poetry.

Cactus to lizard, cups of sand, hands shading eyes against the reductive light: the desert's declining evening, the sky exactly in the middle.

A field of smiling rubber flowers.

Vast animal nights no longer the stuff of unnecessary fictions.

They spent those warm summer evenings in drink and
dissipation, growing fat and soft on the warm writings of lazy
poets while drooping eyes and fluttering fingers caressed
merciless fountain pens.

Animated skeletons scoff at the notion of rest, relentless in their
insatiable appetites, scornful of rhyme and measure, desperate
for narrative, they ask, "why are we so dry?"

It was simply the way such things were done in the South.

The politics of slippery exposures to reveal flesh.

"Je suis toujours seul, même avec toi," elle dit.

Exposed as.

In moments of blind ambition she imagines writing something
with the word "dune" in it, or perhaps even the plural: *dunes*.

She is discovering the pleasures of being about.

All this time he is staring out the window, "what kind of bird is
that," he asks, "sitting in that tree-like thing over there?"

As if her collection were a genre all its own, for it was indeed a
collection—a collection of sentences; a collection that provided
them with the opportunity to reflect on the sentence itself, and
to ask themselves just what a sentence is or could be and what
it might do to or for them, leading them to inquire more deeply

into their dependency on language and to ask, "just what is our relationship to the sentence?"

Though intent on searching, he found no answers at the bus station.

In the fullness of time she would come to know herself young despite the passing of certain years.

There was no method beyond the readily apparent.

She contemplates with a sort of tender contempt the face of the man sleeping beside her.

As if behind the words an identity lies in wait.

Thought extinguished.

Two days later, along the river, he asks himself if he will remember how to swim when the time comes.

Why else did she imagine a link between boredom and language unless she saw her destiny tied up in the fate of words?

As if she were coming to know herself in the very act of disappearing.

A sharp pencil is a sloped awning, built for the asking.

In the realm of art and literature there comes a point where the greatest pleasure lies in the disappointment of our expectations.

Words plying the mind.

True awareness is the only viable ethical code.

"The biochemical arrangement (some sort of neurological hierarchy) they call my personality, coming into coincidental contact with a series of historical and environmental conditions, results in who I am," she says (and yet she worried: the car she drove, the clothes she wore, the coffee, cigarettes, appropriate amount of leather, her vocabulary, sexual exploits, familiarity with the right drugs, brands of bourbon, handcuffs, political views culled from movies, properly stained paperbacks, the right music—was all this really going to become her way of answering the question of who she was?)

Time will tell, even if there is no one left to hear the story.

The ballet of gazes that passed between them.

Motion is comforting because being still we must confront our demons, while by moving we evade both them and ourselves.

To turn waiting into something else.

Whatever power he has over women is a reflection of the lack of power he has over himself.

The purpose of a confession, even a literary one, should be anything but justification.

If their autobiographical efforts fail to achieve a level of literary interest, it is not because they do not romanticize themselves— obviously they do so constantly—but because they do so in uninteresting ways.

All that time spent with the phonebook was beginning to convince him that poetry was more a matter of knowing how to read than of what someone else wrote.

How can you be sure of anything, and can you rest until you

are sure?

"We must inevitably question the language of poetry," she insists.

He dreams of an arm that reaches out from the pages of the book open on the table in front of him, grabbing his throat and throttling him as he reads.

The slowly built up silt of consciousness.

Not peace, not happiness, not satisfaction or contentment, not even knowledge or truth, not faith or belief, but beyond all this: Hope.

There is little epistemological risk in a flower.

Sounds have no natural connection with our ideas but like shapes they communicate them in a stunning feat of penetration.

He thinks of this as an alchemy gone horribly wrong.

Lines of communication dry like burnt grass housed in oversized cardboard boxes.

If language will not efface the boundary between sacred and profane, then why should he persist in believing that anything important lies on either side of that line (but with only the line to support him, how long can he hope to stand?)?

Mutatis Mundialis

What then of that desire to understand, in whatever form or manifestation it appears, something that at times has been called God and at times has gone by other names or remained unnamed out of respect or fear or an acknowledged failure to understand?

Some gentle velvet moment following this brittle connection disturbs two cans tenuously stretched across a linoleum table and joined by a single piece of string.

Through the window a view of rotting chairs and the whine of two-stroke engines like a thin layer of acoustic filtering.

The sun a harbinger of decay.

It is not the image it evokes but the sound of the word "abyss" that constantly tempts the poet.

She can hear night collapsing, dropped from above or pulled from below.

Of all Calvino's definitions of a classic, the one he likes best is, *a classic is the term given to any book which comes to represent the whole universe, a book on a par with ancient talismans.*

"I do not need to sleep if I am free to hold onto those books you sold me in a dream," she whispers.

Because mankind's experience is not reducible to any set of concepts, the hopeless struggle of the philosopher to do that which is not only impossible, but perhaps even undesirable, is the perfect paradigm for man's struggle to create something meaningful out of the time we have here on this earth.

Singing to her bookshelves, "there is no syntax for your words, no grammar for your punctuation, just the echo of your sounds, you ring in my tiny ear made large in an expanding head swollen at your audacious pleasures; ring on old men, ring on."

As if only beginnings offered an opportunity for future closure.

Now that computers can play chess better than we can, why should we bother, unless our goal is to become more like computers?

Since it is about words that she wonders, shouldn't she be able to find a word for that about which she wonders?

Occasional spasms of pleasure dipped the needle.

There is no audience; we are all on stage.

She returns to the library of her wilder days.

That the page itself might become antiquated flesh.

Silence falls effort ceases time flaps they stop they stand.

Computers can even write poetry, but can they *read* poetry? — this may be the only thing left that we have over them, but of course most of us can't do that either.

Alone again and still.

To be refused.

Dancing skeletons have lost all menace.

Exploring the relationships between things is destructive but not permanent.

If we cannot think outside the constraints of grammar, can we at least conduct our thinking within the awareness of such constraints?

Pride is a sentence awaiting punctuation.

The shopping list included items that were never bought, or were bought at prices for which things were never sold, and it might include places that did not exist, or were never visited on the dates or in the manners described.

It was important that such falsehoods exist.

The voice was not resigned to accident, but committed to it.

A dark and isolate figure.

It was all part of some poor Fragment, the slender Ort of her remainder.

Poetry as a form of thought.

A writing too intimate to be an activity that takes place outside herself.

The whole of language a series of plagiarisms.

The smile wears thin around the edges.

Drowning in their expectations.

Here are four animals each intent upon the consumption of the other.

Intelligence is manifest in the ability to get what one wants, wisdom in the ability to properly determine what that is.

She wanted a second chance; he wanted a repetition of their first chance.

She wanted him to learn from the past before he found someone else to repeat it with.

Organized noodles kinetically digested.

Occasional lollipops drooping past antique children.

Ancestor of chickens.

"A curious case of narrative impotence," she thought, watching him sleep through the alarm yet again.

Church architecture taught him to value cunning irregularity. To break the pentameter, the gothic heave.

A thirst for living tissue created this addiction.

Language not transparent but reflective.

The absence of list.

Lost in the folds of language.

A form of seepage.

Absolute certainty becomes obsolete certainly.

A tendency to notice.

They cannot climb every tree in this world of birds.

His fingers too distant from her need.

He remains the unsolved vessel of the clarification she seeks.

A vague nucleus of energy running to words.

A moon cruelly serene poured down its useless beauty.

Passive acceptance rubs its knuckles against the cool concrete and soon the pavement is awash with blood.

For months he lived on Altoids, coffee, vitamin C, and the hope that she would call.

No documentation is required for this brief passing.

Joining him, she too felt fine under the table although cheated of the coveted view by its insidious architecture.

His body a deformed cartridge packed with soggy powder.

Paris has become a stationary famine.

Skepticism as a kind of tourism.

The infinite migration of desire from one object to the next.

Green upon yellow they draw their vocabularies from different wells yielding the same water.

To free ourselves from those observations that lacerate our being.

Writing for her was still mostly waiting.

She was not interested in plot, character development or storytelling, but in condensation, in the reduction of expression by means of revision.

The voice that remembers in the absence of the void.

Mold grows on damp socks.

War is like large sperm.

Lethal burden of contemplation.

Immense silence.

She dreamed that it was too late to be in love, even though it was he who had pushed her in front of the train as she craned her neck to catch a glimpse of the clock whose existence he had been caught fervently denying.

A degree of paranoia conducive to her creative impulses.

Her logic was not very well behaved.

Poetics is a question of what we do with poems, aesthetics a question of what they do with us.

The waiter wavered on the fringe of her peripheral vision preying on the empty cups and saucers, while she, guiltily moving her pen back and forth across the page, measured out the distance between hand and I.

Poetry he might think of as an invitation.

Such delicate writing might not stand up to being read.

Practice without repetition.

An economy all their own in which his vocabulary is not even legal tender.

What most people call errands he sees as the insurmountable obstacles of daily living.

A man of exuberant appetites; he would devour the world, though it be hers.

His knees trembled at the mere thought of her.

Longing to disintegrate.

Sizable portions.

Aberration of intent.

Agents of melancholy plumbing the dimensions of regret.

A hope he dared not share with the hoped for.

She sees herself perched on the knees of marble giants sunk to the bottom of the sea.

His eyes moved across the covers of truculent magazines whose lush images tempted him to be young, thin, beautiful, rich, loved, and uniquely the same as everyone else.

Exposed but not forgotten.

The man taking pictures was part of the art.

They sat talking in the ill-lit cafe, one of them wondering if sexual tension was mounting.

Each book was a mirror casting back at him a distorted image of a misconception.

She sought to transfix him with that look described by Proust as *the comprehensive gaze with which, on the day of his departure, a traveler hopes to bear away with him in memory a landscape he is leaving for ever.*

Hoping to see a reflection of his own secret thoughts, he saw instead a record of the expectations he had discarded with each turning page.

He watches the mysterious patterns her hands weave in the air before him, but whether their motion is a threat or an encouragement he is too drunk to tell.

Plotting the death of flies.

No such thing as an innocent book.

Caught in the net of their own circumspection.

She was not speaking, yet she stood before him resplendent in the act of articulation.

Violent urges.

In yellow, green, and gold, her words sound like bells beneath the water's surface, deprived of oxygen.

Her trembling thumb beckoned to the passing motorists who, either blind to her urgency or overcome by their own (which basically amounts to the same thing), sped by with indifferent velocity.

He imagined the Othellian rage he would display at her bedside, dispensing his thunderbolts of recrimination like a syphilitic Zeus.

She who made the brazen world golden.

The mind, forced by the bullying influence of connectivity, flits from one enslaved association to another.

While she spoke of a great thing that comes at us like a beast.

So flexible it seems lewd in the darkness.

No end in sight.

Nor a legitimate beginning.

Old men on park benches mumbling prayers beneath false beards.

Same wavelength, but out of sync.

The wave of an effortless flow of language washing over her.

To see again in each of these quiet days that flash of the blonde color come to be associated with lonely nights.

First he called it an abstraction, then truth, because it was permanent.

She could never see the law directly but only its expression.

There is no present like the one you imagined in the past.

"Today in the garden it seemed to me as if the roses were real, but their red was fake."

They walk home together, taking their unsteady way past the quietly beckoning houses.

Not for them the solicitudes of comfort or the reassurances of being home.

Their mouths found each other in the dark and suddenly it was light all over.

Faithful unto the forgery of experience.

Flesh of creativity.

She left him to dwell in those palaces of his mind evacuated by her parting.

In writing it is often hard to tell which is the disease and which the drug.

The thrall that curls around a measure of precaution.

Solipsism is an answer to a question no one asks.

How then to reconcile their piercing stares with the opacity of the world?

His desire both a perpetrator and a victim of her calculated repetitions.

What doesn't change is the distance.

She wants to reach out past the steering wheel, through the windshield, and efface that distance.

As if through the leaves the sky is a shared opportunity.

She sought a letter not already in use by other words or writers.

You don't judge a book by its cover, but a man by his books.

She writes poetry in order to provide prose with an exterior life.

Every day was a celebration of one thing or another.

Of lusty words that drifted through his orbit he quickly lopped their wanton growth.

She offers him as an example of simile: "like a photograph taken by the camera of my imagination on the film of language."

A revolution is a revolution in language: a change in poetry.

Constantly in danger of disappearing over the precipice of signification.

Gripped by a beauty bordering on the pathological.

Things they had forgotten how to be responsible for the knowing of.

Today the future is premature.

The past, recallable or not, can never alleviate the weight of being alive; only add to it.

This touch is already a memory.

He treated objects like women.

They keep making the same mistakes over and over, only with different people.

A moment of yellow from someone else's book.

Even if she cannot believe that poetry will change the world, she feels it is her highest responsibility to live in accordance with the faith that says it will (in other words, the artist must remain committed to a faith in which she does not believe, and artistic production takes place from within this doubt, not in denial or in ignorance of it).

Available for inclination but eager to decline.

She has shown him that the truest autobiographies are composed in other people's words.

What she calls "a history of construction."

Self-knowledge then is so difficult not simply because it is a matter of figuring out who we are, but also because it includes discovering what we hope to become; it is endless because self-knowledge includes our potential as well as our actuality.

He saw the shreds of clothing fluttering on the line between birds' feet as the yellow haze which had drenched the South for decades made its way North.

Can poetic language be a form of logos?

The passion of thought is fundamental to its thinking.

Writing is a form of waging.

Their relationship a dedicated monument of waiting.

Dim memories of a noise that aligns itself with the alluvial flow of remorse and the stark whispers of ambition arise amid the cluck of disapproving tongues.

He suspects that there will be an art of the future, but he is not sure he will have understood the past well enough to be able to appreciate it.

So long as its articulation does not extend beyond its own operating system it serves their purpose well enough.

For the time being she stares out the window into the ambiguous sky through smudged paw prints left behind by the cat.

As their mutual distances grew he sought refuge in alcohol's ability, not to distract his attention, but to obliterate it.

The continuing advent.

He followed her, leaving his park bench and the joys and sorrows of park bench existence behind him.

He thinks of reading as that form of Eros that searches restlessly for those other parts of the self we have lost or perhaps never had.

She writes the names on scraps of paper and in carefully annotated notebooks, for these names are spells.

That poetry might teach him to drive his mind.

The pleasure of lawnmowers and vacuums.

His hand rests on her knee as he gently steers the car through the parking lot.

From alluvial sludge to astral plain.

Books and art present us with occasions to lose ourselves and occasions to discover ourselves, and life presents us with occasions on which sometimes one, sometimes the other, is more desirable.

He feels they are running out of time, but for what?

Forgetting is necessary for survival, but recalling the act of forgetting hurts all over again.

"We keep making the same mistakes until we learn something about ourselves that we thought we were going to find out about the world outside us."

"Treat this too like a museum," she suggests, pointing vaguely at her chest as if to say, "love makes the world go round, but such revolutions hurt like hell."

She left him to reign in his meager corner of the relentless material world undaunted.

Not merely victims of Proust's *cold government of reason*, but witnesses as well.

Eventually they had to evacuate the premises.

He feels the inevitability of those mistakes he'll make again once she's gone; and then she closed the door and was gone.

And then it was over in a slow, sad, quiet way, and nobody was going to kill anybody, there would be nothing dramatic; it was simply over.

So many failures do not finally add up to success, they just mark the passing time.

Void of expression.

Language is just another word for nothing left to say.

But reading is not merely a means to an end because there is no end.

Enough ambiguity to cancel out coincidence.

It was all preparation, but for what?

A first step we must take over and over again.

And yet knowing when to stop is as hard as getting started.

Stories woven from the frayed fabric of previous stories.

Each word rises.

Stories without beginning or end.

Remote.

Ever unfolding.

(1994-2007)

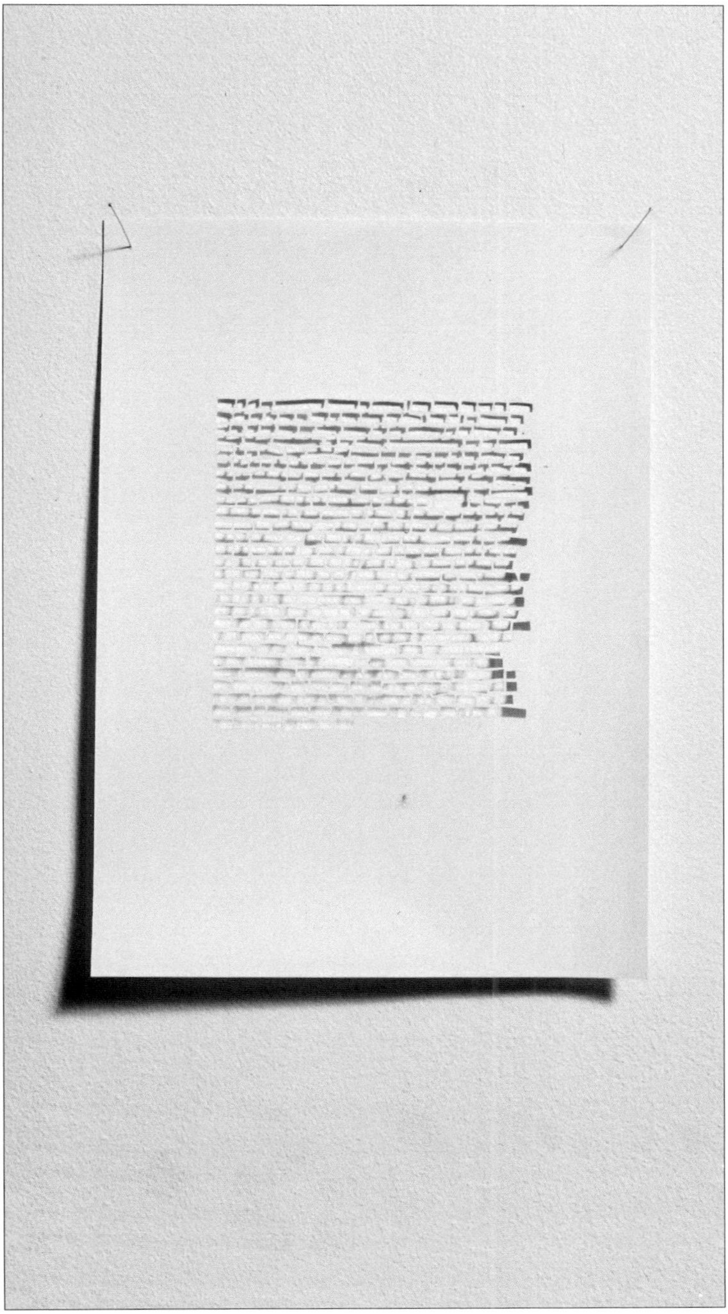

Colophon

The visual work in this book was provided by Swedish artist Mathias Kristersson. 100 copies of the first edition include five loose photographs by the same artist. Additionally, 5 copies of this book have been reserved for the artist to incorporate in his visual practice at a later date.

On page 3:
BOOKCASE WITH PHOTOGRAPH
31" x 50" x 11"
2008

On page 179:
FIVE POEMS ABOUT BOREDOM AND LONGING (detail)
5 A4-size paper sheets, with words cut out in a pile on the floor.
Installation approximately 10 feet.
2007

Photographs by Mika Korhonen.